Dax Franklin walked away from his marriage a few years back thinking that it would save Jory Carters' career, a career he had fostered himself. Years later, when Dax hears that Jory is in a coma, he comes back, realizing he has never stopped loving him.

Jory needs rehab, but his manager boyfriend has other plans. Dax is willing to help Jory through his struggle with alcohol and drugs, but it must be Jory's decision.

Is the memory of what they once meant to each other enough to save Jory from himself, or will his status as an international star prove stronger?

This book is a work of fiction. Names, characters, places, and incidents either are products of the author's imagination or are used fictitiously. Any resemblance to actual events or locales or persons, living or dead, is entirely coincidental.

Over My Shoulder
Copyright © 2019 D.J. Manly
ISBN: 978-1-4874-2588-3
Cover art by Martine Jardin

Published by eXtasy Books Inc or
Devine Destinies, an imprint of eXtasy Books Inc

Look for us online at:
www.eXtasybooks.com or www.devinedestinies.com

OVER MY SHOULDER

BY

D.J. MANLY

CHAPTER ONE

The screen door opened. Susan Carter stood there, holding a mug of steaming coffee in her hand. She put it down in front of him and pulled her cardigan around her. "Getting colder," she said, taking a seat opposite him on the lawn swing.

Dax sucked in some of the frosty air. "You're right. Winter is coming."

Susan reached over and covered his hand with hers. They didn't speak.

"When he recovers, I want him to come home for a while," she said. "He used to love sitting out here on summer evenings, especially after the porch was screened in, no bugs, you know."

Dax met her gaze. He watched the tears fill her eyes. "He'll sit here again," he insisted. "I know it."

"Ben called me." She made a face.

Dax didn't comment.

"He's not happy you're back."

"I know."

"You are still married. Ben can't prevent you from being there. You could keep him away from Jory if you wanted. You could—"

"Susan." Dax interrupted. "Jory chose to be with Ben. They live together now. I have no right to prevent him from being there with Jory." Dax sat back in his seat and closed his eyes a moment.

"He's the reason Jory is in a coma." Susan's voice shook

1

with anger and she let go of his hand. "He pushed him too hard, Dax, just like he did with you."

Dax raked a hand through his hair. He was exhausted, both physically and emotionally. He hadn't felt like this in a long time, not since his days of touring with the band. The flight had been long, and there were delays. He'd been frantic, worried about Jory, desperately combing the internet for any news.

Jory Carter has fallen off the stage during a homecoming concert in New York.

He'd tried reaching Susan, but there was no answer at the house, and he didn't have her cell phone number any longer.

At the hospital, he met only with frustration. He couldn't get anywhere near the front desk. Security guards and reporters surrounded the hospital. Dax had been delegated to the hallway for two hours before he spotted Jory's mother hurrying down the corridor, a tissue bunched in her fist.

Dax elbowed his way through the reporters who had descended on her like a pack of starving wolves. With the sunglasses, beard, and baseball cap, he hadn't been recognized. He managed to finally pull her off into one of the washrooms, barricading the door behind them.

He removed the hat and sunglasses. She looked stunned when she realized who had hold of her arm. "Dax?"

Dax braced himself, not sure how she would react to seeing him again. After a few seconds, she burst into tears and put her arms around him. "Dax, oh Dax, thank God you've come."

Susan released him. "There are so many questions, but there will be time for that later."

"How is he?" Dax scanned her face.

"In a coma. He fell off the stage, hit his head. They don't know if he's going to ever wake up." Tears rolled down her cheeks. "He was exhausted, Dax. And he's been drinking, too, a lot. I'm sure he is headed the same way —"

He swallowed.

She squeezed his arm. "You know when you left without a word, Jory was devastated."

"I was convinced it was for the best at the time."

"Thanks to Ben." She met his gaze. "Ben wanted Jory for himself. He would have done anything to get rid of you because Jory would have moved heaven and earth for you. He loved you so much, Dax."

Dax noted the use of the past tense. "I was in a vulnerable state. I didn't want to hurt Jory's career. Mine was over, but his was just beginning."

"Whatever possessed Jory to get romantically involved with that man?"

That was the one thing he didn't want to get into. "I need to see Jory, but I can't seem to get anywhere near him."

"You are still legally married." Susan sniffed. "They have to let you see him."

When the swarm of reporters was finally whisked away by hospital security, Dax made another attempt to see Jory.

"You're Dax Franklin." The nurse gasped. "You haven't changed except the hair is shorter and you have a beard. Oh my God," she said, putting her hand over her mouth, "I love you."

He gave her a faint smile. "Thank you. Can I see Jory now?"

She nodded, leading him down the hallway. She was chattering all the way about what songs she had loved and how everyone thought he was dead.

"I'm not dead," he said, pausing at the intensive care room she took him to.

She came closer. "It was so romantic, your wedding. I couldn't believe it, Dax Franklin and Jory Carter, two of the hottest—"

He put up a hand. "Can we talk about this later?"

The young nurse nodded. "Of course. That's his manager in there, Ben Lennox." She drew closer, whispering, "His boyfriend now."

"Yes, I know who he is," Dax said, thanking her, then walking into the room.

Ben Lennox was standing by Jory's bedside. He was fit, well dressed, tanned. He'd bleached his hair out to a sandy blond and had added a nose stud. *Forty going on twenty.*

When Ben saw Dax, he took a step back. The look on his face was not one of welcome. "Susan said you were back. You don't need to be here."

"Hello, Ben," Dax said, his gaze going to Jory, lying there with an oxygen mask fixed over his face, hooked up to all kinds of things. Dax closed his eyes. This was a nightmare.

"You have no right to be here now." Ben pointed at him.

Dax held up his left hand, indicating the gold band on his ring finger. He'd never taken it off. "I could ask *you* to leave, Ben."

"Jory and I are together now," he said. "We're a couple." He took Jory's motionless hand. "We tried to find you. Jory wants a divorce so that we can get married." Ben glared at him. "Now, that may never happen."

"I was easy enough to find," Dax said, coming closer to the bed.

Ben let go of Jory's hand. "He's over you. He has a new life now. He won't want to see you. I'll look after him."

Dax nodded. "I see you've done a bang up job, Ben, making sure he was taking the right pills to keep him going, had the finest whiskey, the best cocaine." Dax met his gaze.

"What happened to you, Dax, was all your doing, none of mine. You were the hottest rock star on the planet, and you threw it all away by getting wasted every night." Ben shook his head. "That's all on you. The only decent thing you ever did in your sorry, miserable life, was to leave Jory. Why don't you go back to wherever you were and to whomever you were fucking, and leave Jory and me alone?"

Dax stopped listening. He stood looking down at the man he loved, a single tear rolling down his face. Jory was so still, lying as if already dead. He should have stayed. He should have been around to protect Jory from Ben. He leaned over and kissed his forehead, smoothing back some of his hair. "I'm here," he whispered.

"Touching," Ben said. "Just remember, you're his husband in name only. As soon as Jory is on his feet, we'll be serving you with the divorce papers."

Dax turned and looked at him. "If Jory comes out of this and he wants a divorce, he'll have it, but he will be the one to ask me, not you."

Ben muttered something and walked out of the room.

Dax turned to look at Jory again. He leaned down and whispered into his ear. "You're going to come out of this, baby. You're going to be all right. I love you. I never stopped." He kissed him gently on the cheek. "I'll be back."

Susan insisted Dax come home with her. They returned together to the house where Jory had grown up. Dax ate sparingly. No appetite. He sat outside on the lawn swing, drinking endless cups of coffee. Susan urged him to sleep. He tried. Sleep just wouldn't come.

He mulled around Jory's room, staring at the old posters of his former self on the wall, dressed in leather, holding his guitar. They had laughed about those posters after they'd gotten together.

"I've always been in love with you," Jory had told him one night as they lay in Jory's bed at his mom's. They'd come for a visit, and Susan insisted they stay there, huddled together in Jory's three-quarter bed.

Dax stared up at his own image on the ceiling, teasing Jory about jacking off as he looked up at it.

5

"Damn right, I did." Jory cuddled closer. "And now I've got the real thing. So, get to work."

Dax closed his eyes and got up off the bed, a sob at the back of his throat. He came downstairs. Susan was sitting on the sofa with a photo album on her knee.

"Look," she said, moving the album so Dax could see, "your wedding photos. It was so windy that day on the beach. Look at my hair."

Dax glanced at the photo. Susan stood in between Jory and himself, big smiles, hugging.

"Your hair looked great," Dax said. He'd been halfway to being plastered and they'd only been married two hours. He'd passed out on their wedding night. Jory had forgiven him, but he'd been disappointed. Jory had this thing about not fucking until they were legal. It had driven Dax nuts, having to wait for Jory to be completely his. But when Jory finally gave himself totally, he couldn't get enough. God, they'd had the best sex.

"Dax," Susan said, "I've lost you."

"Sorry." He shook himself. He didn't want to look at those pictures. "Did Jory tell you he wanted a divorce? I wouldn't blame him if he did, I was just wondering if he ever mentioned it?"

"No, not to me," she said. "After you left, he fell into a deep depression. He went on tour, and it seemed he just wanted to work, work, work. Ben took advantage of his vulnerability, caught Jory on the rebound."

Dax recalled when he'd first heard that Jory and Ben had hooked up. He'd tried to avoid reading the celebrity news for a long time. Then he saw their faces plastered on a magazine in Canada at the grocery store. *Jory is over Dax, says manager, Ben Lennox is the love of his life.* It had hit him like a bolt of lightning—god, anyone but Ben Lennox.

Susan was still talking. Dax focused on her words, putting

his feelings aside. "I couldn't get him to even say your name, Dax. He never spoke of you. I guess there was too much pain."

There was a long silence between them.

Susan met his gaze. "Did you ever think to pick up the phone and tell Jory you were all right?"

"I didn't think it was a good idea, thought it would derail him, thought if I heard his voice, I wouldn't be able to help myself. I'd get on the first flight I could and fly back to him. He deserved his shot at fame without me to complicate things."

"Dax, I truly believe it was hard for you to leave him, and that you thought you were doing it for Jory, but Jory thought you'd deserted him. You were sick. You left the hospital against the doctor's orders. Jory came back to tell you that he was putting the tour on hold to be with you and you were gone. No note, nothing. He was absolutely devastated." Tears ran down her face.

Dax bit into his bottom lip. "I know I hurt him deeply. I don't expect him to forgive me. I was vulnerable and easy to manipulate, confused. I thought I was doing the right thing, and the more I got away from the cameras and the circus of what my life had become, the less I wanted to come back to it. You're right, leaving Jory broke my heart."

"If this hadn't happened, if Jory wasn't in that coma, would you have ever come back?"

He didn't know the answer to that. He took a deep breath.

"Ben is wrong for Jory, and you know it. You know it better than anyone, Dax."

He nodded. "Yes, but if Jory wants to marry Ben," Dax said finally, "I can't stand in his way." He met Susan's gaze. "No matter how you feel about Ben, Susan, it has to be Jory who decides."

She looked away.

He knew she wasn't pleased with his answer. "I'm going to spend the night at the hospital with Jory," he said. "I'll wait until Ben leaves."

"I'll drive you." She got to her feet. "I want to see him again."

Jory remained in a coma for more than three weeks. Then one morning, he just woke up.

Dax had spent most nights there, asleep in the chair, holding his hand, only leaving when Ben showed up. He'd go back to Susan's, take a shower, sometimes sleep a bit and eat. Then he'd come back to stay at Jory's side.

When Dax saw Jory's eyes open, he let out a cry. "He's awake!" He went to tell someone at the front desk.

The nurses came rushing in, and a few minutes later, the doctor was there, looking into Jory's eyes with a light and asking him questions.

"What's your name?" the doctor asked.

"Jory Carter," he said. His gaze kept straying to Dax, who stood a few feet away.

The doctor glanced at Dax, then at Jory. "Do you know who that is?"

"My husband, Dax Franklin."

Dax smiled at him.

Jory looked away.

"Looks good," the doctor said to Dax. "We'll have to do some tests to make sure. I'll be back."

Dax waited until the doctor had left the room, then moved closer to the bed. "How do you feel, Jory?"

"Like I've been run over by a truck," he said, looking at him. "It's really you."

"Yes," Dax said. "It's me."

"You look, holy shit, you look so fuckin' beautiful," he whispered, his eyes bright with tears. One rolled down his cheek. "Healthy. Are you all right?"

"I'm not drinking if that's what you mean. It's been over two years now."

"I hate you," he whispered, then turned his head away.

Dax nodded, swallowing hard. "Okay, you're entitled to. I didn't come back to give you grief, Jory. I heard about the accident and —"

"Thought you'd have to plan a funeral?" He looked at him again, smirking.

"Don't even joke about that shit."

"Well, you're still the executor of my will so I guess you'd have to do that shit."

"Well, there's no need now. Listen, I know you're with Ben. I've tried to give him his time with you."

"What a gentleman you are," Jory muttered. It sounded like a sneer.

"Do you want to marry him?" That was tough to ask but he had to know.

"Hell, no," Jory said. "I'm not doing that again, ever."

Dax nodded. "Okay but I'll sign the —"

Just then, Ben came running in. "Baby, oh God, Jory, I'm so happy to see you awake." Ben leaned down to kiss him.

Dax left the room. He went to sit in the waiting room. The stress of the last few weeks had been the greatest test of his sobriety. He hadn't wanted a drink, and that was a miracle.

Three years ago, he'd almost died. In fact, the doctors told him that it was his last chance to get sober.

You're young and strong, Dax, but you're not immortal. If you don't stop drinking now, in a few years, you'll be dead.

As he'd lain there in that hospital room, he couldn't help but wonder how in the hell he'd gotten to this place. He had everything he could possibly want, fame, fortune, music awards, and love. God, Jory was the best thing that had ever happened to him. He'd done all he could to get him that record contract and now his career was taking off. And even with all that, he couldn't stop drinking. There were the drugs, too. He'd smashed up several cars, forgot to show up for concerts, and said stupid things to reporters and in front of cameras. It seemed that he was always under the influence.

It took him time to realize that it was a disease, one he'd inherited from his father, who died when Dax was five. And then there was Ben. The first thing you learn in therapy is that you, and you alone, are responsible for your drinking. He could blame the life, he could blame his friends, and he could blame Ben. But he couldn't change them. He could only change himself.

He'd always avoided drinking too much because of his dad. And he'd never taken drugs, not until Ben gave him those pills that night in Detroit. He was seventeen and the band was on the threshold of success. They were opening for some big-name rock group and Dax was super tired. Their schedule had been insane. He felt as if he couldn't get up on that stage anymore. It took so much energy. He should have said no, refused to take what Ben offered.

Ben said the pills were harmless, caffeine, he'd said. So, Dax took them with a bit of liquor to wash them down with. The combination of whiskey and uppers gave him a high like no other. Ben always had what he needed when he needed it. As their success grew, so did the pressure. Sex with strangers, all night parties, and arenas filled with screaming fans, it eventually left him feeling empty. The high he got on the stage was replaced by the high he got from drugs and booze. It wasn't until he met Jory that he began to feel as if his life had meaning again.

He shook himself. He didn't want to think about the past but here he was, right back in the muck. News had gotten out that he was back and spending his time at the hospital. Suddenly he was hounded by reporters again. The headlines screamed *Dax Franklin has come back from the dead to declare his love for Jory. Who will Jory choose?* So far, he'd managed to avoid answering any questions.

The gossip rags proclaimed, *love triangle, what will Jory do now that his hunky, ex-rocker husband, has come home? Will Dax resume his career? Is he still strung out? What is he doing here? Fans say they belong together.*

Photos of their wedding five years ago were plastered all over the covers of magazines and on television talk shows. People who'd known him, former members of the band, a woman claiming she'd been Dax Franklin's housekeeper. God, the list went on and on. They all had something to say about him and Jory.

Susan arrived in the waiting room. She was so happy about Jory being awake. She hugged Dax. "He's going to be all right."

"I know. That's wonderful news," Dax said.

"The doctor will come in to talk with us in a few minutes," she said. "Dax, listen, I need your support."

He narrowed his eyes.

"Ben wants to take Jory back to LA. I want him to come home for a little while. Ben can't take care of him properly and I want to be with him now."

Dax shook his head. "It will be up to Jory, Susan."

"Will you stay a while longer?"

"Ah, Susan, I—"

She put up a hand. "Don't say anything yet. It's just that he's going to need to go to drug therapy. Who better to support him through that, than you?"

"Is that for sure?" Dax quirked an eyebrow.

"He had traces of illegal substances in his bloodstream when they brought him in." Susan chewed her nail. "The life, you know, he's got a drug and alcohol problem. Ben doesn't help."

Ben walked in. He looked over at Susan. "Did I hear my name?"

Susan looked away.

"Jory is going to be fine now," he said to Susan, ignoring Dax. "They will release him in a few days, I think. I'll hire a full-time nurse and — "

Susan began to protest but then fell silent as the doctor walked in. He was a short, white-haired gentleman with glasses. He looked at Susan and Dax. "He's lucky," the doctor told them. "I'd like to keep him for a day or two more, run a few tests, then I'll discharge him. He does need a drug counselor."

Ben interrupted. "I'm hiring a nurse, and I'll get him the best LA has to offer. He needs to manage his drinking."

The doctor looked at him. "No, Mr. Lennox, he needs to stop drinking altogether and doing hard drugs. He needs counseling, rehab."

"Of course, that's what I meant," Ben muttered.

"Ben," Susan said, "I want Jory to come home."

"Home? LA is his home," Ben objected. "He's not a little boy anymore, Susan. He's twenty-four years old."

"He needs a break from that world, and you won't have a lot of time to spend with him," Susan insisted. "You go on tour with your other singers. It would be better if he were away from those influences for a while."

"It would be best if Jory kept his distance from the party crowd for a while," Dax said. "I could be his sponsor if he stayed. He could do this as an out-patient."

Ben was livid. "You, sponsor Jory? Fuck you," he muttered. "That's never going to happen."

"It will be up to Jory," Dax said in a calm voice.

The doctor looked at Dax. "I think that's an excellent idea, Mr. Franklin. If you can get Jory to agree, I'll set it up here at the hospital. The sooner we get started, the better. You people work it out."

The doctor walked out. Susan followed, wanting to continue the discussion with the doctor.

"Are you really serious?" Ben hissed at Dax like a snake. "There is really no need to waste your time here. Do you want to help Jory, or fuck him?"

"Long way to come just for a fuck, don't you think?" Dax shook his head. "I offered to help, that's all."

"All you've managed to do is upset him."

Dax met his gaze. "If that's true, I'll leave. All Jory needs to do is tell me to leave. I'll go."

"Good," Ben muttered. "The sooner, the better. Jory is coming home to LA."

"Is that the best for him, or for you?"

"You being here is making everything rain shit," Ben grunted.

"If you are so secure Ben, so sure that Jory loves you, why are you freaking out about me coming back here?"

"When Jory met you, he was innocent, only seventeen. He was enthralled by that rock star persona, the tight leather pants, and the guitar riffs. He didn't know who you really were inside. Now you've got nothing to offer him. You're just a washed up, has been."

Dax smiled at him. "And what were you enthralled by when you offered to manage the band, Ben, when you tried to get me to give you a blow job in the back of the tour bus when I was seventeen? I wasn't famous then."

Ben's face paled. "Fuck . . . you," he sputtered. "You're a liar. You were a full of yourself two-bit guitarist who was just lucky to have a pretty face and a tight little ass."

Ben's words had no power over him anymore. Dax just laughed.

"Now I'm going to see about setting up things for my man when I take him back home in a few days." Ben looked at his phone. "Enjoy these last moments with him."

"You're going to have a fight on your hands, Ben. Susan won't have it."

"Susan can go to hell, and so can you." Ben stalked out, almost knocking a nurse off her feet.

Dax decided he should go to see Jory, find out what he wanted to do. If he were needed here a little while longer, he'd call Freda. She could run the club without him.

Susan and Jory were deep in discussion when he walked in. He almost walked out again, but Susan heard him and turned to look at him. "Come here," she said, holding out her hand.

He took it and came closer, meeting Jory's beautiful brown eyes.

"Jory and I have been discussing a few things," she said, standing. "Jory needs to make some decisions. I'll leave you to talk."

They were alone. Jory looked at him for a long time before speaking. Finally, he said, "I guess you know Mom wants me to stay in New York."

"Yes. I think it's a good idea, too," Dax said.

"Away from Hollywood."

"Yes." Dax nodded.

"Ben wants me in LA."

"It doesn't matter," Dax said. "It's what you want, not Susan or Ben."

"Or you? What do you want?" Jory asked.

"I want you to get well," Dax said sincerely.

"Mom says you'll stay in New York at the house, support me through this shit."

Before Dax could reply, Jory put up a hand, adding, "I really don't need therapy."

"Oh," Dax said. "And how did you come to that conclusion?"

"I can just stop. I overdid it, you know?" He lifted his

shoulders in a shrug.

"Sounds familiar." Dax sat down in the chair beside the bed.

"I'm sure you're not comparing me to you," he muttered. "You were a mess. You almost died."

"Ah, reality check." Dax waved his hand around. "You just woke up from a coma."

"Listen, you can't just come in here and act like my husband and start telling me what to do." His voice was calm, but there was strength in his tone.

"You know I've never done that. Do you want me to leave?"

"Leave where?" he asked.

"Here, New York?"

"I don't care what you do." He looked away.

"I told your mother I'd help you through this. If you don't want my help, fine, go to LA with Ben." Dax looked down at his hands.

"Ben is not the devil."

"I never said he was. And I'm not judging you." He got up and looked out the window. It was raining.

"Deep down, you think I'm a fool for getting involved with Ben. When did you know we were together?"

"Doesn't matter." Dax turned around. "I understand why it happened. I blame myself for everything. But if Ben is the man who makes you happy, then okay. Just remember he's also your manager. His success depends on yours. Does he love you enough to take a loss on your career?"

"There won't be any loss," Jory protested. "I'll be back on tour. It's just being put off for a few weeks."

Dax's eyes widened. "A few weeks?" He turned to look at him. "Are you serious? You won't be strong enough physically or otherwise to be back on tour in a few weeks."

"Look, I never forgot what you did for me, Dax. You made

me. I wouldn't be where I am today if you hadn't used your influence. But it's been a few years since you've been out there. Maybe you don't understand anymore."

"Understand?" Dax shook his head. "I understand all too well."

"So" — Jory cleared his throat — "if I go back to LA, you're leaving the US."

"I have a business in Vancouver, a business partner."

"What's his name? Is he good in bed?"

"It's a he turned she actually, name is Freda, and it's nothing like that. We met in rehab. We are good friends. I fronted the money for the club and decided to become her partner. That's it."

"Don't tell me there's no one?" Jory met and held his gaze.

"I haven't taken a vow of celibacy if that's what you mean, but it's always been you," Dax told him. "There's no one else." He held up his hand, smiled. "Still married."

Jory nodded silently. He looked away.

"So, listen." Dax handed him a slip of paper with a phone number on it. "This is my cell phone number. If you need me, call me."

"Wow, your phone number. That's something." Jory studied the paper.

"You decide what you want to do." Dax headed to the door. "If you go to your mom's, I'll stick around while you're in rehab. If you go to LA, then I'm going back to my life. Do what's best for you. You already know what I think." Dax lifted a hand and walked out of the room.

CHAPTER TWO

Jory settled into the seat by the window and looked out at the JFK airport. The sky was cloudy today, and it was cold. He could feel winter in the air. He missed the snow living in LA. He missed a lot of things.

Ben was on the phone, marching up and down the aisle of his private jet. It was a familiar scene. He was the busiest music promoter in the business. He lived and breathed the music world.

Jory closed his eyes. His mother was angry with him. She had hounded him right up to the last minute to stay in New York. "You need to come home," she insisted.

In his other ear was Ben, reminding him that he was a grown man, too old to be running back to Mommy. "You need to be in LA. Your life is there. I'm there. Baby. Did you ask Dax for a divorce? We could have a June wedding. We could . . ."

No. He wasn't going to marry Ben.

Divorce? Divorce Dax? Would that do any good? Would that make him stop thinking about him, stop aching for him? He doubted it.

When he'd opened his eyes in that hospital room and seen Dax standing a few feet away, for a moment, he thought he'd died. He was in heaven now. All he'd asked of heaven was the chance to look at Dax Franklin for eternity. And there he was. He hadn't changed. He looked even better, healthy, so strong and sexy.

Three years, nothing, although he knew Dax was alive and

well, living in Canada. Jory had hired a private detective to track him down. "Don't approach him," Jory had said, "just want to know that he is okay." Of course, no one knew that, not Dax nor Ben, nor his mom. Whenever Ben would suggest Jory find Dax and ask for a divorce, Jory would say he was working on locating him.

Ben put down the phone now and came to sit beside him as the plane taxied the runway.

"Problems?" Jory asked.

Ben took his hand. "Complaints from that new band, The Riders, something about the stage set-up in Munich. Nothing to worry about. How are you?"

"Okay. Think I'll take a nap."

"Good idea," he said, stroking his hair. "Don't worry about your mom. She'll come around. Ah, when was the last time you saw Dax Franklin?"

"Can we please drop that subject?"

"Just asking."

"Two days ago at the hospital."

"And you have his address now so you can serve him with the papers?" Ben met his gaze.

God damn it. That again. "I'm sure Mom knows. Look, when things settle down and Mom gets over being pissed at me, I'll ask her for it. I'm sure he's gone now anyway."

"Um." Ben settled into the seat. "Seems to me that your mom has always been overly stuck on Dax Franklin. You'd think she was a groupie." He laughed.

Jory eyed him. "Dax always treated my mom well. She liked him. He was charming and generous with her. And who wasn't a fan of Dax? He was the greatest guitarist ever. No one is better on the guitar than Dax Franklin."

"Dime a dozen, guitar players," Ben scoffed.

"No." Jory looked at him. "I know you don't like him, Ben, but whatever you say about Dax, you cannot deny his talent.

18

Come on?"

Ben sighed. "Okay, you're right. He was one of the best guitar players in the business. But that's history now."

"Only because he chooses it to be." Jory glanced out the window.

"I'm sorry the hell you lived with him. It won't be like that with us." Ben squeezed his hand.

Jory said nothing. It wasn't hell. There were times when it was extreme happiness, unbelievable passion. There were moments when Jory thought he was gliding on clouds. Dax could make him feel euphoric. Loving Dax was a roller coaster ride, and when Dax left, Jory hit the cement so hard he thought he'd never get back up again.

Dax was love, and laughter, and sunshine, and craziness, and passion. God, passion. No man had ever made him feel like Dax had in bed. Dax had been his rock, he'd believed in him, supported him, and used every contact he had to promote him.

When Dax collapsed that last time on stage, Jory canceled his shows, came flying back from London to be with him. He didn't care what Ben said, or the music company, or the lawyers. His career be damned. There was nothing more important to him than Dax, his husband, the man he adored, even if their marriage had been on the rocks the last few months because of Dax's drinking.

That night, the last night in the hospital with Dax, Jory had told him, "I love you so much. We can do this together, baby, we'll get through this. The hell with my career, I don't care about that. I want to be with you. Let's start over."

When he'd come back to the hospital the next day, and Dax was gone, his entire world had gone out from under him.

Jory closed his eyes. He had to put Dax behind him. Seeing him again had revived all those feelings. In the hospital, he found himself holding his breath until Dax came back into the room. It was like he was seventeen again. He resented the fact that Dax could still make his heart pound like a drum in his chest.

If he'd stayed at his mom's, Dax would have been there. He'd be too close. It would be so easy to fall back into his arms, to make love to him with everything he had. Too damn easy.

He'd made the right choice. He could just say no to the bottle, no to the drugs. He didn't need counseling, and he didn't need Dax.

Back at Ben's luxury condo in Beverly Hills, he wandered around as if he was in a foreign place. He stared out the window at the clear blue sky and wondered when he'd feel as he had before he'd lost three weeks of his life.

Ben came into the living room and wrapped his arms around him. "Hey, I got you a nurse."

"I don't need a nurse, Ben." He looked at him. "I'm fine, really. What I need is something good to eat. What's Walter cooking in the kitchen?"

"I thought we'd go out to dinner. Some of our friends want to see you, babe. And it's good to be out and about so the press can grab a few photos."

Jory groaned. "Really?"

"Listen, we don't want rumors. We want your fans to know you're fine and that all that stupidity about Dax Franklin is not true."

"What stupidity? What did they say about Dax?" Jory picked up his phone.

Ben took it away. "Nothing. It's just that he's been out of it so long. The press wants an interview. He comes running back when he found out you were in the hospital. It looks weird."

"What did they say?" Jory asked. "I'm going to find out

anyway."

Ben handed his phone back to him. "Go ahead, read. I've got an errand to run." He pecked his cheek. "Be back soon. Rest up before dinner."

"But I—" Jory began. Ben was gone. The last thing he wanted tonight was to be out in public. Damn. He flung himself into a chair and googled his name. Everywhere he was, Dax was, too. It was strange to read about the description of your life and feelings written by someone you'd never met. And the comments by the fans were lively.

Joryfan — I love Jory, love his beautiful songs, love ballads, all born of pain and passion . . . for Dax. What a beautiful love story. They have to get back together.

Daxforever — Dax Franklin, yum, why in the hell would Jory choose Ben over Dax? Is he blind? Dax is one beautiful man, and so talented. I still have his posters on my wall. Did you see the pic of him snapped outside the hospital? He's so hot with that beard.

Jorynumberonefangirl — Dax dumped Jory and disappeared long ago, now he comes back like a white knight. You got to be kidding. Yes, Dax is hot, but Jory was right to give him the boot.

Daxforever — You don't know what you're talking about. Dax made Jory Carter. He'd be just another guy playing piano in some bar somewhere if Dax hadn't of given him a hand. Jory owes Dax everything. Come back, Dax. We miss you. We love you. Don't give up on Jory. You made him so happy. We want you together. We want to hear that magical guitar.

Jory put down the phone. Enough of that. The talk would die down eventually. He was impressed at how Dax had managed to avoid getting interviewed. He'd always been good at giving the paparazzi the slip. Jory remembered when they'd first met, the night Jory and his friends, Martin and Katlin, had snuck into that dance club downtown with fake identification cards. Dax Franklin had walked into the one club in

New York City where all the celebrities went, a club fashioned on the famous Studio 54.

There had been a buzz of electric excitement sweeping the crowd the night Dax Franklin, lead guitarist for Intoxication, had walked into that dance club. It made Jory and his friends feel as if they'd just won the lottery twice.

It was hard enough to get into this club as it was, now, he was in the same room with Dax Franklin?

"Could be bullshit," Martin told Jory and Katlin, having to yell over the music. Then suddenly, the song stopped right in the middle and the latest hit by Intoxication started to play. Nope. Dax Franklin had to be in the room.

"They're playing it because he's here," Katlin screamed in excitement as she jumped up and down, dancing to the beat.

"Let's find him," Martin insisted. "I'm dying to see if he's as hot in person as he is on my wall."

They tried to elbow their way through the crowd. The minutes and then hours ticked by and they gave up on getting anywhere near him. There were too many people.

"Never mind." Katlin laughed. "At least we're breathing the same air as he is."

"Not good enough," Martin said. "I want to see him."

"Me, too," Jory said, disappointed. "Can't afford to go to a damn concert. Anyway, wait here. I'm going to the bathroom. We'll try again."

What would have happened if he hadn't had to take a pee then? He and Dax would have never met. He wouldn't be an international star. He wouldn't have a broken heart either.

He got to the bathroom, used it, and was washing his hands when this huge guy barged in. He pointed at him. "Stay there," he said.

Jory narrowed his eyes, then just as he was about to protest, he came face to face with Dax Franklin. His jaw dropped. He was speechless. He heard a booming voice outside say, "Out of order. Find another one."

"Hello," Dax said, smiling. "Hope my bodyguard didn't freak you out."

Jory gripped the sink. He had a deep voice. Beautiful. That was all he could think. Dax Franklin was beautiful. And he was there, standing a few feet away from him.

"Gotta take a wicked pee," he said, moving over to the urinals.

Jory swallowed.

Dax turned around, unzipped. After he'd peed, he zipped up his jeans, then looked at him. "What's your name?"

"Name? I have a name, yes," he said.

Dax laughed. "Yeah? So, what is it?"

"What's what?"

"Your name?" He grinned, cocking his head.

"Dax Franklin," Jory murmured.

"Same as mine. That's quite a coincidence." He started to laugh.

"What is?"

"Your name is Dax Franklin." He folded his arms across his chest. He was wearing a blue t-shirt, a short, black leather jacket, and tight, ripped jeans.

"What? Oh, no. My name is Jory."

"I like it," he said. "Do you know a back way outta' here, Jory?"

"Yes, the alley. Might set off an alarm. Why?"

"I need to get away from the paparazzi. They're all over the place." He lowered his head and whispered, "They want to know all my secrets."

"Do you have a lot of secrets?" Jory met his gaze. Damn, those eyes.

He grinned. "Maybe. How old are you?"

He stuck up his head. "Old enough to get—"

"A fake ID?" He raised an eyebrow. He was too damn cute.

Jory smiled. "Something like that."

"Want to come with me?"

"Yeah, yes, for sure. Where?" Jory was breathless.

"Anywhere. Let's go." Dax grabbed his arm and pulled him out of the bathroom.

Jory wasn't sure why Dax Franklin would invite him to go anywhere, but he didn't care. He felt high. They rode around all night in his sports car, eventually sitting in a park until the sun came up, talking—just talking.

"So"—Dax leaned back on the bench, his dark hair in his eyes, long legs stretched out—"who are you, Jory Carter?"

"No one," he said.

"You're someone. What do you like to do?"

Look at you, Jory wanted to tell him. What I'd like to do is touch your hair, kiss your mouth, and go crazy on that incredible body of yours but I'm good just looking at you. Instead, he said, "Ah, I sing a little."

"Yeah, cool," he said. "You play, too?"

"Piano. My mom made me take piano lessons as a kid. I hated it then, but now, I don't know, I like to write songs, so piano helps."

"So, sing me one of your songs."

"No way," Jory said.

"Why not?" He nudged him.

"You're Dax Franklin."

He grinned. "So? I'm sure you're good."

"How would you know?" Jory challenged.

"Are we still talking about music?" Dax teased.

Jory looked down, embarrassed. "Stop it. You are a big flirt."

Dax laughed. "I know."

"You sing to me," Jory urged.

"No. I'm off stage now."

"What's it like?" Jory asked him. "Being you?"

"Tiresome," Dax said. He reached over and pushed some hair off Jory's forehead. "I like being here with you. It's quiet. Peaceful. No one wants anything from me. Tell me one song you wrote."

"I don't have a melody, only words."

"What are the words?" Dax asked. "Come on, indulge me."

"Ah, okay, um, love waits to spin me round and round. I can't wait to leave the ground. Are you the one to take me on the wind? Take me on the wind, I never want to land. Lay me in the sand and be my love. Lame, eh?"

They were looking at each other then. Something happened, neither one was sure what it was.

Dax spoke first, breaking the spell. "Not lame. That's beautiful. I wish I had my guitar. I'm sure I could put a melody to that." He started to hum something and then Jory, under his spell, melted into those eyes as Dax sang Jory's own words back to him. It was genius. He was a genius.

"Was that my song?" Jory blinked.

"Yeah. It's good. Keep working on it."

"You sing like an angel."

Dax laughed out loud. "Haven't been called that before. I'm not a singer. I'm a guitar player."

"I know you usually only sing backup. Luke is lead singer, but you sing well."

"Thanks. I prefer my guitar." He took his hand. "You have the fingers of a piano player."

Jory felt his pulses race. Dax Franklin was holding his hand. "You have the fingers of a guitar player, and the ah . . . arms."

Dax laughed.

When Jory noticed it was almost eight o'clock in the morning, he said, "Shit, I have an exam first class. I have to be in school."

"College?" Dax lifted an eyebrow, with a sheepish grin.

"You know, don't you?" Jory looked at the grass, embarrassed. "I suppose you think I'm just a little kid."

"A baby," Dax teased.

"You're only twenty-one," Jory accused, "not so old."

"Sometimes I feel ancient," he said. "What else do you know about me, Jory?"

"You were raised in Los Angeles by your uncle. Your dad died young, and your mother remarried. You have a reputation."

"Do I now?" he mocked. "I'm a bad boy?"

"Definitely. You like to raise hell, but you are also generous and sweet. You give a lot of money to hospitals that treat sick children and to animal shelters."

"And you like that?"

"I like everything about you," Jory told him. Wow, had he said that? "Guess I should go."

"Come on. I'll take you to school," Dax offered. "Which way?"

Before Jory got out of the car, Dax grabbed his hand. "So, when is your birthday?" he asked.

"In two weeks," Jory told him. "Why?"

"So, I don't get arrested when I try to kiss you," he told him.

Jory was speechless. Then Jory said, "You know, I won't tell if you try. I mean, I won't—"

Dax leaned over and kissed him on the forehead. "I'm in enough trouble for other shit. I'll pass on the corruption of a minor bit." He pressed a piece of paper into his hand. "My cell phone number. Call me if you ever want to come to a concert. We're playing in Boston in two weeks."

"Really? Cause I can't afford your—my mom is a single parent, and we'd have to get to Boston and—"

"You won't have to pay, Jory," he said. "I'll make sure you get there, and that you have a place to stay. Bring your friends, your mom, too. You gotta' go now," he said. "The bell is ringing."

"Oh yeah, okay." Jory took one long look at him, jumped out of the car, and raced into the school.

Suddenly a voice cut into his daydream.

"You're not ready yet?"

Jory looked up to see Ben standing in front of him. "Ready for what?"

"Dinner reservations are at six."

"Why so early?" Jory asked, looking at the time. It was almost five.

"You'll see. It's a bit of a welcome back at the hotel."

Jory groaned. "Not a party. I'm not up to that."

"We won't stay long," Ben said, pulling him to his feet. "What have you been doing?"

"Nothing and I like it."

"Come on, put something nice on," Ben said. "We won't stay late."

Later that night, there were many people around him. There were flashbulbs and microphones. Someone kept passing him champagne. His head hurt. It was almost midnight when Ben came to sit beside him again. He'd been hobnobbing with the press and music people most of the night. He put his arm around Jory. "You okay?" Ben picked up an empty champagne glass. "You only had one, right?"

"I can't remember how many," Jory said, getting to his feet. "I need the bathroom."

Ben didn't hear him. Some music producer came by the table, and Ben started talking to him. As Jory made his way to the bathroom, people stopped him to talk, asking him how he was doing. He smiled like always and said, "Fine, fine," then moved on again. Everything was spinning.

He wanted to leave. He felt sick, drunk. He'd promised

himself one glass, and he'd had a dozen. He left the bathroom and headed to the lobby. He looked at the doorman. They'd brought his sports car tonight, but Ben had driven. He walked up to the man who parked the cars. "Have someone bring my car around," Jory told the man at the door as he stumbled outside. Ben could find his own way home.

"I don't think it's a good idea, sir," the man said, following him outside. "Wasn't Mr. Lennox driving?"

"It's my fuckin' car." Jory pointed at him. "I want my God damned car."

"Let me call Mr. Lennox, sir, and —"

"Fuck Mr. Lennox!" Jory took a swing at the man and missed. Everything was blurry. He kept walking, out of the parking lot, down the street. He needed something, someone. There had to be someone somewhere who would have a drink with him, who didn't know who he was.

He walked into the first tavern he found, sidled up to the bar and threw a hundred-dollar bill down in front of the bartender. "Drinks for everyone!" he cried out, raising his arms. He pulled another wad of hundreds out of his wallet. "Plenty more where that came from. Let's party!"

That was the last thing he remembered. When he opened his eyes, he was lying on a cold floor. He lifted his head. Pain, ouch. He raised a hand to his head. It was sticky with blood. He had no clothes on, and there were empty bottles all around him. The only other piece of furniture in the room was an old cast iron bed.

"Where in the fuck am I?" Jory muttered. He stumbled to his feet. It was daytime. He looked out the window. He didn't recognize anything. "Where are my clothes?" His wallet was there, but his credit cards and cash were gone. His cell phone was missing, too.

He staggered over to the bathroom, dirty, smelly, the toilet full of something. "Gross." He looked in the mirror — dried blood on his face. In the bathtub was someone's old pants and a shirt, a tattered pair of canvas running shoes.

He'd have to put those on if he wanted to get out of here, but outta' where? He needed a phone. Had he driven here? No. His car was back at the hotel with Ben.

He donned the dirty old clothes and left the room, feeling his skin crawl. God only knows what he'd catch from these rags. He slowly descended the stairs to the front desk. There was an old man there with no teeth, gumming a toothpick. "If you got a complaint, don't bother," he told him.

"Ah, listen, I need a phone." Jory was shaking all over.

"Pay phone in the hall." He hooked a thumb in that direction.

"No, I have no money."

The old man stared at him. "This is a business. Not a charity. You owe me money. Let's see, three nights, that will be—"

"Three what?" Jory looked at him. "No. I couldn't have been here three nights. It's Friday."

"Yeah, now it's Tuesday." He pointed at him. "Three nights."

"Where are we?"

"At the Sleep Well Hotel. It's on the sign." He pointed outside.

"Where is the . . . where?"

"Slab City."

Slab city had once been the site of a former Marine Corps base. Now it was mainly a place to get lost, nothing but a long stretch of beach. How in the world had he gotten here?

"Now, you owe me—" The man was saying.

"Listen, I'm Jory Carter. Do you know who that is?"

"Some celebrity I suppose, singer boy. So what?" the old man scoffed. "You're not the first famous person I've seen down here, drinking their lives away."

"Let me use the phone for free, and I'll give you what I owe you, plus five hundred dollars."

The old man shrugged. "Come on." He took him into the back room. "If you bull shit me, I'll put a hit on you. Phone is there."

"Do you remember who brought me here?"

"Two men and a woman, that's all I know. You guys partied on down."

Jory closed his eyes. "Can I have some privacy please?"

He glared at him. "You steal anything and I'll . . ."

"Five minutes."

In his wallet, he still had the number of his car service. He took it out. When he did, something else fell out onto the floor. He picked it up. It was Dax's cell phone number. He stared at it, put his face in his hands. He was scared. He'd woken up in a dive. Someone had hit him, robbed him. God knows what else they'd done to him. And he'd lost three days, three days he couldn't remember.

Tears ran down his face. He put the two numbers side by side. Car service would take him back to Ben, Dax's number would take him where, to New York? He wasn't sure. He made his choice. With shaking fingers, he dialed the number and waited for someone to pick up on the other end.

It rang three times. He almost hung up. Then, he heard Dax's voice. "Hello?"

"Dax?" he said in a shaky voice.

"Jory? Are you all right? What's going on?"

He started to cry, and for a few minutes, he couldn't stop.

On the other end, Dax kept telling him it was all right. "Jory. Where are you? Tell me. Where are you?"

Finally, Jory got control, and he said, "Dax, I'm scared. I've lost three days. I'm in a strange place, and they robbed me. I have no clothes."

"Can you call your drug sponsor?"

"That's what I'm doing now?"

"What? I thought Ben was going to set you up with counseling?"

"I want to come home to New York." He sniffed. "I need help. I need you. Dax, please. Say you'll help me."

"God damn it, I'm at the airport. I'm about to fly to Vancouver."

"Please, Dax, I need you. Stay with me."

"I'll cancel my flight," Dax replied.

Jory breathed a sigh of relief.

"Can you get to the airport?"

"I have no money. I don't want to call the car service because then Ben will know. He'll try and talk me out of it. I don't want him to know until I get home, okay?"

"Of course, but doesn't he wonder where you are? You've been gone three days."

"He wouldn't call the police because it would be bad publicity. And, well, it's happened before."

"Seriously? Jesus Christ, Jory," Dax muttered. "Okay, give me the address where you are. I'll send a taxi, pay it with my credit card and book your flight to New York. I'll have the driver stop so that you can get a pay as you go phone, as well as a prepaid credit card."

"Okay."

"What's the address there?"

"I'll ask the man. Dax, I'm in these tattered clothes. What if someone sees me, the press or something? How am I going to explain it?"

"Tell the taxi to stop at a clothing store and get some clothes with the credit card I'll buy for you."

"Dax, I'll pay you back for all this," Jory said. He was so embarrassed. He'd never been this low.

"Don't worry about that. Get the address of the hotel."

Jory asked the old man the address, then told Dax.

"That sounds like Slab City," Dax replied.

"Yeah."

"Wow. Okay."

"And I owe this guy three nights and five hundred dollars," Jory added.

"What's the five hundred dollars for?"

"For using the phone," Jory muttered.

"A real humanitarian. Fine, put him on the phone," Dax told him. "I'll pay him."

Two hours later, Jory was at the airport with a cell phone, new clothes, and a prepaid credit card. He called Dax as soon as he arrived.

"I'm texting you a screenshot of your ticket. Flight leaves in two hours," Dax said. "It's direct, five and a half hours. You'll land around eight o'clock this evening, New York time."

"Does Mom know I'm coming home yet?"

"Yes, I called her. She's relieved."

"I'll understand, Dax, if you can't stay. Maybe I just need some time at home," Jory said.

"God damn you, Jory," Dax replied. "Don't fuck with me now. I've changed all my plans for you. You are going to rehab. And that's final."

Jory swallowed. "Okay, okay, whatever. I said, yes, as long as it's as an out-patient and you agree to be my sponsor."

"You really are not in a bargaining position right now, Jory." Dax sounded irritated. "We'll talk about it when you get home."

"All right."

"Listen, I booked you an aisle seat near the bathroom just in case and try to drink a lot of water before boarding, also take some ibuprofen in case. I've taken many a flight with a hangover. It can be hell."

"Thanks."

"You should call your credit card company, let them know your cards have been stolen."

"Shit, I never even thought of that."

"The sooner, the better," Dax advised. "I'll rent a car, be there when you get in. See you soon." The phone went dead.

Jory had bought a baseball cap and some dark sunglasses. He tried to keep a low profile. He didn't want to talk to anyone. He drank a bottle of water and took some headache medication. When he was seated on the plane, he closed his eyes. He was tired. He just wanted to sleep. He kept looking for a text message to pop up from Dax. There were none.

When the steward went by with the cart, he heard him say, "This flight includes a complimentary drink. Would you like something, sir?"

Maybe something to take the edge off. One drink would fix the pounding in his head. It felt like someone was hammering with a drill at the top of his skull. "Ah, yes, thank you. Gin, a little water."

CHAPTER THREE

A beige baseball cap and dark sunglasses couldn't disguise Dax Franklin completely, but at least it caused people to hesitate before approaching him. It was cold today in New York, the snow formed an inconsistent pattern on people's lawns, and left tree branches looking like someone had crocheted little coats for them.

He didn't much care for the cold. Now it looked like he'd be spending the winter here. Poor Freda. The club was swamped with tourists. "How much longer, Dax?" she asked him on the other end of the line.

"I don't know, a few months. It depends on how it goes with Jory."

"You still love him. I hope he appreciates what you are sacrificing, darling. I know so many men who would snap you up in a heartbeat. I think it's a mistake."

"Look, Freda, I owe him. We're still married. And, I feel responsible for this somehow."

"Dax, you forgot what we learned in rehab. Who is responsible for Jory Carter's drinking?"

"I know, we can't change others, just ourselves. But what if I hadn't helped Jory build his career? He wouldn't have gotten involved with Ben. Maybe it was because I left him without even saying goodbye, Freda."

"Dax, baby. You were sick. You needed help, and you didn't want to be a burden to Jory. You left so he could go on with his career. You thought you were doing the right thing at the time. The past is the past. That's why I don't think you sticking around is a good idea."

"I can't abandon him a second time. I won't do it. He says he needs me. I'll get him through this, and then I'll come home. Hire some more staff. We can afford it. Katy can help manage the club with you."

"Of course, but I miss you. Okay, please call me at least three times a day, okay?"

He laughed. "Okay. Thanks. Love you," he said and hung up.

His friendship with Freda had become the most important thing in his life over the past three years. When they met in rehab, she was just as big a mess as he was. She'd come from a rich family. She had a big allowance that she'd all but wasted on drugs and booze. Her family was paying for rehab.

"This is the third and final time," Freda had told Dax soon after they met. "They sent me here, their transsexual, drunken son, turned daughter. We're at the dirty little secret rehab center, honey."

Freda knew who he was of course, as did the others at the center, but no one gushed over him or demanded his autograph. Here, he was just another addict, trying to get well.

Freda knew almost everything there was to know about him, and he, her. She told him that her dream was to own a nightclub. Dax had no dreams left, so he piggybacked on hers. He fronted the money, and they became partners.

Freda joked about how the club would be their constant test. Surrounded by alcohol every day, the temptation to drink was always there, especially when things went bad. They'd both stayed sober, attending their meetings like religious zealots going to church. They had each other, too, and of course, Dax no longer had the stress of being an international star.

"Don't tell me you don't miss it, sweetie," Freda had said to him one night after a meeting. "It must have been a rush, a high, all those people adoring you."

"I don't miss that," Dax said. "The only thing I miss is play-ing my music for people. If I could do that without all the bull-shit, then I'd be happy."

"Why not do it at the Club?" she asked. "We could feature live bands. You could get up and play guitar whenever you want to."

It was a great idea, and it filled a void in him, that anxious feeling that gnawed at his gut because he needed to play, to have people hear him play. But the void that Jory left in him was always there. He wondered if he'd ever love again. He tried, went out with a few guys, even slept with a few, but he couldn't feel enough for them. Affection. He liked them. He wanted them physically, but Jory lingered at the back of his mind.

"If he missed you so badly, honey, wouldn't Jory try to con-tact you?" Freda asked him one night after she'd found out he'd stop seeing someone.

"What does breaking up with Nico have to do with Jory?" he asked her, wiping off the bar.

"Everything," Freda said, taking off her hoop earrings. "You told Nico you were still married. Why not get divorced? Jory is not banging down your door. And don't tell me it's because he doesn't know where you are." She pointed at him. "He can find you if he wants. You're not hiding."

"I'm not ready. Let's leave it at that, okay?"

"He's living with his manager, Dax, the same idiot who helped put you into rehab." Freda shook her head, pulling her thick black hair out of a ponytail. "He's moved on. He's not wasting his time moaning about you."

Dax looked at her. "You're right. I know that."

Freda came up and hugged him. "I love you, kid, but you need to put the past in the past."

He was tired now, sitting in the airport, waiting for Jory to arrive. Maybe Freda was right. Maybe he should have told Jory no. He'd offered before, and Jory chose Ben. Was he wasting his time? Damn it.

When he saw Jory walking toward him, Dax got to his feet. The closer Jory got, the more Dax noticed that Jory wasn't walking straight. Damn it.

"Hey," Jory said, smiling. "Aren't you a sight for sore eyes? Is that the sweater I bought you when we were in Hong Kong? You always looked so delicious in red, Dax." He reached up to touch Dax's face, and Dax gently pushed his hand away.

"You're drunk," Dax accused. "How much did you drink on the plane?"

"I had a few drinks, just to take the edge off. Damn it, Dax, my head was so bad. I took four of those painkillers, like candy."

"I bet," Dax said. "Come on." He adjusted the hat on Jory's head, then handed him his sunglasses. "Put these on. Let's get out of here." He took Jory's arm, hurrying him along to the exit.

"Why so fast, why we in a hurry?" he demanded.

"You want people to see you like that?" Dax demanded, dragging Jory outside.

"I don't give a shit," he said.

"You will. Come on."

When Dax put Jory into the front seat and fastened his seatbelt, he breathed a sigh of relief. They'd gotten some curious stares, but no one had stopped them. When Dax got behind the wheel, Jory announced, "I'll drive if you want."

Dax looked at him. "Yeah, right. I don't think so."

He shrugged. "Do you know what happened to my car?"

"What car now?" Dax pulled out of the parking space.

"The car I was driving."

"In LA?"

"Yeah, right, I'm in New York now." He smiled. "Oh, Ben

has it. Never mind."

A few minutes later, Jory had passed out in the front seat. Dax turned the radio on low and left the airport. With the traffic, it would take at least an hour and a half to get back to Brooklyn. One of Jory's songs came on the radio, and he turned it up. His voice was sweet, pure, that was the first thing that Dax had noticed about it, and he had great talent in writing lyrics. Jory had written this song when their marriage was on the rocks. He couldn't recall the title.

Time stands still when I'm not in your arms. You stand on the precipice of my heart. Hold me like before, and it will be all right. I'll never leave your side. Baby, I need you tonight.

Dax switched it off. It was painful. His drinking was out of control then. Jory was always on the road. They talked about separating, and then they'd meet and have this mind-rocking sex and it would begin again.

Now, here he was, Jory passed out beside him, heading into a new journey, one he wasn't sure he should be taking.

Words they'd spoken to each other, always knowing it should end but not being able to end it, played in his head.

I don't want to get back on the crazy ride with you, Jory. We're no good for one another.

I know. Just stay with me tonight, Dax. I don't know how to let you go.

That was the problem. Neither one had seemed to be able to let go.

Dax saw the exit for Brooklyn. They'd be back at Susan's by eleven. He was thinking about Ben as he drove into the driveway and the fact that he didn't know where Jory was.

Susan had the lights on. She was standing at the door, waiting.

Someone needed to call him. Despite Dax's feelings for Ben, it wasn't right not to tell him that Jory was all right.

Dax turned off the engine. He came over to the passenger side and got Jory out of the car. He half carried him inside.

"Is he drunk?" Susan asked, helping Dax when they came inside.

"Of course," Dax said, pulling him down the hallway. "I'll take him upstairs. Come on, Jory, one foot in front of the other, okay?"

It took over ten minutes to get him upstairs. In Jory's room, Susan took over, and Dax went back downstairs. Dax was sitting at the counter, drinking a glass of water when Susan walked in.

"I got him half undressed and under the covers. He's really out of it. Is he all right?"

"No, he's an addict. He couldn't even stop drinking on the plane despite his hangover. Susan, he lost three days. Someone stole his clothes, his credit cards. He doesn't even remember what happened."

"He should have never gone back to LA, Dax," Susan said, shaking her head.

"I think he knows that now."

"I want to thank you for coming back here, Dax. If I haven't told you, I—"

He put up a hand. "Why do you think I can save him, Susan? Do you know what those last six months were like before I left the US?"

"I know it was bad, you were drinking and taking drugs, you were putting on shows in different parts of the country, but you tried to work it out. Despite everything, you didn't split up."

Dax sighed, closing his eyes. "We hurt each other deeply, but we were as addicted to each other as I was to the bottle. This isn't going to be easy because there is a lot of history between Jory and me. He's drinking his pain away like I drank mine. As he heals, gets sober, a lot of feelings will bubble to the surface. I have to protect myself, too, Susan. I've been two years sober. I need to stay that way. This situation may not be healthy for me."

She touched his hand. "So, maybe he should go to rehab, and you should go back to your life. I have only been thinking about Jory and myself. I'm sorry, Dax."

Tears lit his eyes. He pushed them away. "I need to get some sleep. We'll talk about it tomorrow. You should call Ben tonight before he contacts the police."

Susan nodded. "What should I tell him?"

"Just tell him that Jory decided to come home for a while and we'll take it from there." Dax stood. He kissed her cheek. "Try not to worry. The fact that he decided on his own to come home is a good thing."

She hugged him, and they said goodnight.

As much as he tried, Dax couldn't sleep. Jory was worse off than he'd imagined. He was so angry at Ben for letting Jory get to this point. He was torn. Should he stay or go? If Jory went into a good rehab for a few months, there would be no reason for him to stay. But he knew that if Jory insisted, he'd be here. It was just the way it was.

When his head hit the pillow, he closed his eyes.

He was walking on the beach with Jory, hand in hand. They hadn't been married too long then, and Dax had promised to go on the wagon. He would manage it, sometimes for weeks at a time. When it was just the two of them, no reporters and arenas, it was fine. But as soon as he was back on the road, he'd be drinking again.

Jory got so angry at him one night. He'd been on tour with the band. It was before Jory got his first hit. He came backstage, and Dax was drinking. A couple of groupies were putting the bottle to Dax's mouth. One young woman was moving her hand up Dax's thigh.

Jory grabbed her arm. "Get out," he said. He pushed another groupie out the door, too. The members of the band and some of the roadies filed out without being asked. Jory was in a rage.

"What the fuck, Dax?" he demanded. "You promised. You haven't drunk a drop for two months. Damn it. And who is the whore

with the skin-tight clothes?"

"Calm down, baby," Dax told him. "I don't know her, just a fangirl. And I only drank a little tiny bit." Dax staggered up to his feet.

"Yeah, looks like it," Jory muttered.

Dax reached for him. Jory pushed him away. "Sober up, then come to me. You'd have a hard time getting it up in that state."

Dax's eyes opened, and he sat up. "Jory?"

"Yeah." He heard his voice. He was in the room with him, sitting on the chair opposite the pull-out bed.

"Are you all right?" Dax rubbed a hand over his face.

"I'm sorry," he said. "I fucked up. Again."

Dax sat up in bed. "It happens." He laughed a little. "Pay back for all the times I fucked up."

"Right," Jory replied.

"Jory," Dax said, putting his feet on the floor. He still had his jeans on, but he'd taken off his shirt. "You may need to be in rehab."

"You're going to abandon me then?"

"No. I'd never do that."

"You did, remember?" Jory replied. "I can't do this without you, and I won't."

"Why not? To punish me?"

"Maybe. Maybe I want you to feel what I felt when you left me."

"You think leaving that hospital was easy?"

"I don't know. Was it? Was it easy to leave me and forget I existed?" Jory stood and looked out the window.

"Is that what you think? You think I forgot you? What in the hell do you think I'm doing here?" Dax demanded, standing.

Jory turned to look at him. "Guilt? I want you to stay because you want to, not because you feel as if me, being a loser drunk, is your fault."

"You're not a loser drunk, but it's not my fault you're drinking is out of control."

"Fine, make your decision, Dax. Decide to be here because you care or leave me, again. You are an expert at it." Jory walked out of the room.

Damn it. Dax went after him. In the hallway, he took his arm and pulled him around to face it. "I know you want to hurt me. I don't blame you. But know this, Jory, I left because the last six months of our marriage was hell. It would have hurt your career if I'd stayed. It wasn't the time to put things on hold. I know the business well enough."

"That's not you talking." Jory yanked his arm away. "That's Ben."

"Yes, Ben. He convinced me to leave, but some of the things he said made sense even if it was because he wanted me out of the way so that he could have you."

"I don't think Ben is that calculating. He was concerned about me, that's all."

"Bullshit," Dax said softly. "Anyway, it doesn't matter now." Dax's voice hardened. "I guess you weren't too torn up about me leaving though."

"What does that mean?"

"I'm not the one who fell into Ben's bed right after I left." Jory looked away. "It wasn't like that."

"It was exactly like that. He was the last man you should have been fucking. You knew that he gave me pills, never discouraged my drinking. He only cared about how much money he was making every time I got up on that stage with the band."

"I thought you took responsibility for your drinking. You seem to be blaming Ben."

"I'm not blaming him. I'm just pointing out that he never was concerned about my welfare. He wanted the money, and he wanted you. That was it."

Jory fell silent.

"I don't want to fight about this," Dax said. "I'm going to bed. Ultimately, it's you who will decide what to do. I told you, if you want me to stay, I will. But make up your mind."

Dax walked back down the hallway.

Just before he went back into the den, Jory called out his name.

Dax turned and looked at him.

"You didn't get rid of the tattoo."

"No. I didn't." Jory's name was tattooed right above his heart. "Too much trouble to skin graft," he said.

"Right. I ah . . . well I got yours covered up when Ben and I—well, it was awkward. It made Ben feel, well, you know, especially in bed."

"Even my name on your skin petrifies him," Dax scoffed.

"I thought you would do the same with yours."

"You're there above my heart and you'll stay there," Dax said. "Did you have Ben's name put over mine? The same numbers of letters. Would be easy."

"No," Jory told him, "I didn't. Your names may have the same number of letters, but you're two very different men," Jory replied softly. "Goodnight."

"Goodnight," Dax told him.

When the morning came, Dax got up and took a shower. He pulled on some clean jeans and a navy t-shirt. When he got upstairs, Jory was sitting at the table, the phone to his ear. A cup of coffee was sitting in front of him.

Dax made a signal that he would leave the room, give him some privacy. Jory shook his head, indicating that he should stay.

"When is Mr. Lennox out of the meeting?" Jory asked. "I can't reach his personal number. Okay," he said. "Fine, have him call this number. Fine. Bye." He hung up.

"Can't reach Ben?" Dax poured some coffee into a mug.

"Mom told me this morning she called him last night, left a message," Jory ran a hand through his hair.

Dax came over and refilled his cup.

"Thanks," he said. "Look, if I said anything last night I shouldn't have, I apologize."

Dax shrugged and sat opposite him, sipping the hot brew. "We've said worse to each other. Did you contact your credit card company?"

"Yes, at the airport before I left LA. They've put a hold on it, trying to trace whoever was using it. They spent three hundred dollars."

"Oh, that's not bad. Should we call and see if you can get an appointment with that doctor today, the one who treated you, Dr. Adams?" Dax looked at him.

"So fast?" Jory made a face.

"It will take time to arrange if you still want to do out-patient."

Jory folded his arms across his chest. "I am not going into one of those centers."

Dax nodded. "Okay, well then let's call him."

"Done," Susan announced, walking in the kitchen, holding up a piece of paper. "I called this morning. You have an appointment tomorrow at ten."

Jory groaned. "Thought you were at work?"

"I took the morning off so that I could be with my boys." She came up to Jory and kissed his cheek, then came around and kissed Dax, too. "What do you boys want to eat?"

"Just coffee, Mom, for now, okay?" Jory appealed.

"Don't bother," Dax said. "I'll make a bagel or some toast later. The coffee is great."

"Thanks," she said, pouring herself some. "How's your head, Jory." She came over and began checking his head.

"I told you, it was just a little cut. It stopped bleeding a long time ago. Can we talk about something else? How's your job,

Mom?"

"Busy. The market is hot right now."

Susan Carter sold real estate.

"You know," Susan said. "If you and Dax didn't want to stay here during your treatment, you could be closer to the hospital if you moved into one of my vacant houses temporarily."

"Is that even legal?" Jory made a face.

"It can be done," she said, looking at Dax.

Dax sat back in his seat. Whoa, it was one thing, staying with Jory in his mothers' house, but alone in a house of their own? That was a whole other thing. "It's not that far, Susan, if you don't mind having me here."

"I love having you here," Susan said. Her cell phone rang. "Sorry, that's work. I have to take this." She walked out of the room with the phone to her ear.

Dax realized that Jory was looking at him with a smirk on his face.

"What?" he said.

"You should have seen your face when Mom suggested we move into a house together." Jory laughed aloud. "That scared the shit out of you."

"I'm not scared of that. I just don't think it's necessary, that's all." He finished his coffee. "Besides, I didn't stay so that we could play house together. Ben isn't going to like any of this, so let's not make it worse by moving into a house alone together."

"So, what are we to each other than, Dax?" Jory met his gaze. "Are we friends? Are we spouses? Are we sponsor and addict? How should we define our relationship?"

"Why do we need to define it at all?" Dax asked him, lifting an eyebrow.

Just then, the phone rang. "That's Ben," Jory said, staring at the phone. "He'll be wanting a definition."

"Well then you'd better answer the phone and give him one," Dax replied, walking out of the kitchen. "Whatever you decide is fine with me."

CHAPTER FOUR

The conversation with Ben was not easy. "I still don't understand, Jory," Ben complained on the other end of the line. "Why didn't you call your driver? Why didn't you call me?"

"I was distressed, Ben."

"So, you called Dax Franklin!"

"He offered to help me. I need help, Ben, and being back there with the parties and the people, it's not good for me right now. I almost died. Then I went right out and got wasted again. I got robbed, hit in the head. I lost three days, Ben. I'm not well."

"It's just some self-control you need, that's all."

"I have none. Even after all that, I was drinking on the flight to New York. I was drunk when I got off the plane. Hear me, Ben. I need to be here. Do you love me?"

"You know, I do."

"Then let me get well the way I know how. Here, with my mom, away from the spotlight, the fans."

"And with Dax."

"Dax has been where I am now. He can help me get through this. It's not going to be a cake walk. We may be over, Dax and I, but I trust him. I know he understands what I'm going through. Please, be patient with me. Right now, I feel as if he is the only one who can get me through this."

Ben sighed. "How long are we talking here?"

"As long as it takes. I've got an appointment with the doctor tomorrow. He's going to set things up. I'm trying to pro-crastinate, but Mom and Dax won't let me. I'll call you every night, okay?"

"I'll do what I can to salvage your career. All will be okay, love. Big kisses."

"You, too," he said and hung up.

Jory put his face in his hands. He was tired, and yes, damn it, he could do with a drink. He'd told Ben a half-truth. He needed Dax to help him through this because he'd been through it himself, and yes, he trusted Dax with his life, but the part about them being over? Last night, in the dark, in the hallway, Jory was doing all he could to hold back. He wanted to follow Dax into the den and make love to him so badly. They were over, but damn it, why did he still want him like this?

They'd had great sex when they were together. The sex Ben and he had paled in comparison. The memory of that passion they shared taunted him, especially when he was this close to Dax, his shirt off, still with that tattoo of his name on his chest. He wouldn't cheat on Ben. He smiled, cheat on Ben with his husband. How ironic.

He was laughing when his mother walked back into the kitchen. "What's so funny?" she asked.

"I was just wondering if you could cheat on a boyfriend with your husband."

His mother came over to him and met his gaze. She smirked. "Do you want to cheat on Ben with Dax?"

He laughed again. "It was funny, that's all. No, of course not."

"Dax looks great, doesn't he? He's still as sexy as always, even better now that he's sober, so strong and —"

"Mom." Jory shook his head. "Stop. I'm well aware of that."

She laughed. "Just saying. If I was younger and he was

straight, and —"

"He wasn't your son-in-law?" Jory made a goofy face. "Icky."

They both laughed.

"That would make it odd," his mother said.

"What would make it odd?" Dax asked, walking into the room.

They turned to see him standing a few feet away.

"Nothing," his mother said. "Nothing at all."

"My mom thinks you're eye candy and was prepared to do something very immoral," Jory said, laughing at the horror in his mother's face.

Dax grinned and lifted his eyebrows, reaching out and grabbing his mom. "Oh yeah, tell me in detail."

They were all laughing, and it felt good, like old times.

His mother swatted Dax away. "Stop it."

When the laughter had died down, Jory teased his mother again. "You were so excited when you knew your son was going to marry a rock star. I remember how excited she was, Dax, the first time she met you. Do you remember?"

Dax smiled at his mom. "Yes. She was sweet. She made me a coffee and asked me if I wanted sugar. I said no, and she kept dumping sugar cube after sugar cube into my cup."

"Oh, shut up, you," she said.

"And all the neighbors," Dax added, "peeking over the fence in the garden at me. Remember that girl falling into the rose bushes."

"Karen Delany. Her butt was full of thorns." His mother was howling with laughter now.

Tears were coming down Jory's face. He was laughing so hard. "Mom called everyone she knew and old Mr. Henderson came over with his camera from nineteen fifty. He was trying to grab a picture of Dax and it went off like an explosion. Remember the flash bulb?"

Dax shook his head. "Poor old guy," he said.

"He's got a camera phone now," she said, "but he doesn't know how to use it."

They laughed again.

"That was the same day you guys broke the bed in the attic." His mother pointed to the ceiling.

"We did not break the bed," Jory protested.

"Ah"—Dax put up a hand—"I think we did."

"I was just showing him the old bed." Jory tried to look innocent. "He likes antiques."

"Um"—Dax grinned—"and you wanted me to try it, remember?"

His mom was laughing out loud.

"It was already broken." Jory smiled, then met Dax gaze. "We just ah, put the poor bed out of its misery, while alleviating a little of our own."

Dax shook his head. "Your mother ran up. She thought we were coming through the ceiling."

"My boys," she said, kissing them. "I have to go to work. Be back at supper. Who's cooking?" She looked at Dax.

"I guess I am," he said.

"Hey, I can cook," Jory protested.

His mom and Dax looked at each other, shook their heads, and said in unison, "No."

After she'd gone, Dax asked Jory if he wanted to take a ride.

"Where to?"

"I should go to the grocery store, need a few things for supper. You can stay in the car."

"You dare walk in the grocery store?" Jory asked.

"People don't usually bother me. Sometimes. With a hat and sunglasses, they don't recognize me right away."

"Minus the leather and the guitar," Jory grinned. "Where is your guitar anyway?"

"In Vancouver."

"You still have that collection?"

"Yes, over three hundred now." Dax started writing a list.

"Don't you miss it? It used to be like an extension of your hand?" Jory teased.

"There's the piano here and an old guitar you used to strum on."

"That old thing? Wow, that's ancient. Have you played that since you've been here?"

"No. I played the piano a few times for your mom when you were in the hospital. She plays well, too."

"Yeah."

"Not like you. You're really good."

"Funny how I hated that damn thing when I was a kid. Now, it's my best friend."

Dax folded his list and put it into his pocket.

"Will you play for me later?" Jory asked.

"Sure." He shrugged. "Anything you want."

"Anything?" Jory grinned, looking at him. "Watch it. I could ask you to play naked."

"Wouldn't be the first time."

That was right. Jory laughed. "I'll come with you, but I want to go in. I want to feel like an old married couple doing the groceries together."

Dax rolled his eyes. "Super."

"I'll get my coat."

Jory walked through the living room toward the staircase. He paused, glancing at the cabinet near the window. His mother always kept a bit of brandy in there. It was a cold day. A little nip would take the edge off. He walked over to the cabinet and opened it.

"She got rid of it all when she knew you were coming home," Dax said from behind him.

Jory turned around. "What? I'm not looking for anything.

51

Got rid of what?"

"Jory?" Dax asked. "Come on. It's normal. You want a drink. It's the first thing I used to reach for in the morning, that, and you, of course." He smiled.

Jory slammed the door shut. "I don't want a drink, okay? And I don't want to go down memory lane with you, especially when it comes to our sex life."

Dax looked at the carpet. "Funny, but I cherish those memories." He looked up again.

Jory met his gaze. "Well, I don't whack off to your posters anymore. Sometimes I think you were more a fantasy than anything else. Once you became real, it wasn't as exciting, you know?"

"You don't mean any of that," Dax said. "You're just pissed because you can't find your mom's brandy."

"I know now how to define our relationship, Mr. Franklin," Jory told him, pointing at him. "How about master and slave?"

"Um, great except who's the slave in this equation, you or me?"

"You, master, telling me what I can do and can't do," Jory accused. Damn, he was a grown man. He could drink if he wanted to.

"The only thing you're a slave to is the bottle, my friend." Dax eyed him.

"One drink couldn't hurt," Jory said, his voice softened. "Come on, honey."

"Honey? That's not going to work" Dax took his arm and led him to the closet. "Get your coat."

"It will help take the edge off." Jory took down his coat.

"One drink leads to another drink and to another." Dax shrugged into his jacket. "Come on, let's go shopping like an old married couple."

Jory smiled at him. "If we shop together, then I guess we

will have to sleep together, too."

Dax pushed him toward the door. "You're cheating on me, remember, with your boyfriend?"

"Oh, yeah. Well, it's the hand for you tonight, darling."

Dax didn't comment.

The supermarket was quiet. They walked through the aisles and Jory watched Dax pick up this and that. He as making lasagna. Dax had always liked to cook.

"We need garlic bread," Jory said. "And some nice red wine." Jory picked up an expensive bottle of Merlot.

Dax took it and put it back on the shelf. "Nice try."

"Wine doesn't count."

"I'm afraid it does. Along with alcohol-laced cough syrups."

They headed to the checkout. "Are you telling me that I can no longer drink a glass of wine with my meals?"

"That's what I'm telling you," Dax said, taking out the items.

"What in the hell do you drink with pasta, Kool-Aid?" Jory muttered.

Dax didn't reply.

The cashier smiled at him. "You're Dax Franklin," she said in a low voice.

He put a finger to his lips. "Don't tell."

"Oh God, and Jory Carter? Are you two back together?" She was looking from one to another.

Dax was going to say something, but Jory didn't give him a chance. "We're not really together again. It's just a fucking occasion. Take a look at him, then tell me you blame me?"

The girl's mouth opened.

Dax apologized, took his bag, and pushed Jory out of the store.

Jory was laughing.

"What in the hell is wrong with you?" Dax snapped, putting his bag into the trunk.

"It was a joke. Come on." Jory nudged him.

"I didn't find it very funny." Dax slammed into the car. "You made me feel like a piece of meat."

Jory sighed as he did up his belt. "You'd be prime rib, babe."

Dax wasn't listening.

"I'm sorry. I just feel like I'd like to bite off the head of a snake or something. I feel like I could go screaming through this parking lot. Can't I just have something, a little drink?"

"No," Dax said. "Let's go home. You need to help me."

"Do what?"

"Prepare supper. Grate cheese, cut up stuff." Dax drove out of the parking lot.

"Okay, yippee." Jory looked out the window as Dax drove. He was feeling ill, weak, his mouth watering. His temper was short. He knew it wouldn't take much to set him off.

Back at the house, Dax kept him busy grating cheese. At one point, he threw the cheese grater on the counter and said, "I can't do this anymore. I got to take a piss."

There was a store at the end of the block. They sold wine and beer. He just needed one little drink. A nice bottle of wine for the three of them to go with the lasagna. He got his coat and hurried out the back door.

Ten minutes later, he walked into the store and bought the wine. As he was coming out, there was Dax, standing there, arms crossed. Damn it all to hell. He tried to smile. He held up the bottle. "For dinner to go with the lasagna."

Dax came walking over to him. "Give it to me."

"I'll carry it."

"Give me the wine, Jory." Dax met his gaze. "Do you want to stop drinking or not? If you don't, tell me now."

"So, you can leave me again, you bastard!" Jory accused.

Dax motioned with his hand. "Give me the bottle. If you ever cared for me, ever loved me, give me the bottle?"

"Fuck, fuck you," he said and threw the bottle down on the pavement.

Jory was shaking like a leaf. Dax came up to him, put his hands on his shoulders.

"We're going back into the store, you're going to ask for a broom and a garbage bag, and we're going to pick up all that glass before someone gets hurt."

Jory shook him off. "That coming from a former rock star who used to trash hotel rooms?"

"I never trashed hotel rooms, but I did a lot of shit I had to take responsibility for."

"Like apologizing to everyone you wronged?"

"Yeah."

"You never apologized to me." Jory pushed him away.

"Yes, I have several times. You just don't hear me when I say it."

"I don't accept your apology."

Dax sighed. "That's your choice. Now, do you want some kid to cut themselves on that glass?"

"That's sponsor Dax talking?" he scoffed.

"No, that's responsible citizen Dax talking." Dax met his gaze.

Jory turned and marched into the store. He came out with a broom, dustpan, and garbage bin. Dax stood watching as he picked up all the glass. "Thanks for helping," Jory muttered,

"I didn't throw it on the ground."

Jory went into the store, then came back outside. "Hey, where's the car?"

"I walked. You could use some fresh air."

Jory fell in step beside him. "Friggin' cold out here. Part of my punishment?"

Dax glanced at him. "Maybe. I remember how you hated the cold. Remember that Christmas we spent in the mountains?"

"Oh shit, yeah." He laughed. "Nice cabin, though. Pity we had to leave it to go skiing."

Dax smiled.

Jory punched him. "Why did we go there?"

"The band was playing in Geneva."

"Oh shit, yeah. It was scary skiing down those mountains," Jory said.

"You were on the baby slope," Dax told him with a smirk. "I hardly call what you skied down, a mountain."

Jory rolled his eyes.

As they turned the corner to the house, Jory asked him if he was angry.

"No. Why?"

"Because I left the house, bought the wine."

"It's my job to keep you from drinking, Jory. Tomorrow, we'll have some support. Until then, try to tough it. At least you're not having convulsions."

"Ooh, no. Please."

"It can get that bad for some people. We don't want you to ever get to that point."

Jory squeezed his hand. "You won't let that happen."

"No. I won't," Dax said.

His mother was home when they got there. Dax said nothing to her about their day. Jory was grateful. They ate supper and Jory asked Dax to play something on the guitar.

He obliged him, playing a song that Jory remembered from a few years back. He closed his eyes as Dax sang, remembering how that song made him feel. Dax spent more time playing than singing but this was Dax's song. Jory and his friends had played that video over and over.

He sang along in his head, not wanting to mute the sound

of Dax's voice, so strong and seductive.

Senses overflowing, love so demanding. Being with you always, in my heart. Although we said goodbye, I know until I die, our love will be ... senses overflowing, love so demanding, even in my dreams, I touch your skin ... so love me now while I'm here and ..."

The phone was ringing. It was his cell phone. Ben.

Dax stopped singing.

"Damn it, sorry. I have to get this. I forgot to call him." Jory left the room. "Hey, babe," he said.

"How are you?"

"Okay, wanting to drink but I'm fighting it. Not looking forward to that appointment tomorrow. How are you?"

"I miss you. I want to come to New York, see you."

Jory gripped the phone. "Not yet, okay. Let me get started with the program and then you can come."

"You don't want to see me?" Ben sounded disappointed.

"I just don't want to hear about the music world right now, okay?" Jory glanced into the living room. His mom was playing the piano for Dax.

"Okay, call you tomorrow?"

"Yeah, I'll call you after I see the doctor, tell you what's up."

"Good night, baby. I love you."

"Night, Ben."

He walked back into the room. His mother was playing a lullaby he remembered as a child. He came and sat beside Dax on the sofa. He looked over at Dax a few minutes later, and his eyes were closed.

Susan turned around at the piano. She noticed. "He's tired. Poor Dax." She got up and brought a blanket.

Jory covered him with it, then stood looking at him for a moment. He used to love watching him sleep. "Goodnight, baby," he said softly, leaning over to kiss his forehead.

Jory followed his mother out into the living room. She

looked at him. "You still love him."

Jory bit into his lower lip. "It feels that way at times, but it's born of memory."

"You sure it's just the memories?" His mother looked at him.

"He was mine at one time. He's not anymore. That takes some getting used to, now that he's so close again. We have to re-define the boundaries. I can't just take him in my arms and kiss him whenever I get the urge."

"And you have that urge?" his mother asked coyly.

"Of course. Who wouldn't?" He kissed her cheek. "It's like any addiction. Eventually, you learn to control it just like I'm going to do with the booze. Good night, Mom."

"Good night, son."

"How long are we talking here, until I'm cured?" Jory asked the doctor the following morning.

"It doesn't work like that," Dax said. He'd been beside him the whole time, holding his hand.

The doctor smiled.

"You know what I mean," Jory said.

"Three to four months of daily treatment sessions," the doctor told him. "Then you will have more infrequent visits and of course, meetings."

"Daily?" Jory looked at Dax, then the doctor. "And after that, can I follow up in LA, or do I have to stay here?"

"That's your choice," the doctor told him. "After four months if you are still clean, you can transfer to LA if you want to."

"When can we begin?" Dax asked.

"Wait," Jory said. "That's a big commitment. I'm not sure if—"

"It's not a big commitment," Dax told him. "Three to four months, in exchange for the rest of your life. I call that a sweet deal, wouldn't you, Doc?"

"For sure," the doctor said. "Listen to your husband, Jory. He knows what he's saying. You almost died. And if you continue on that path, you will do irreparable harm to your body. You need to stop now when your body is still young enough to repair itself."

Jory sighed. "Yeah, okay." He looked at Dax. "You'll come with me?"

"Yes, every day," Dax said.

The doctor smiled. "You have some paperwork at the front desk, Mr. Carter. I've tried to hurry the process. You can start as early as tomorrow. Good luck." The doctor shook hands with Jory and Dax and left the room.

Dax looked at him. "Are you ready to do this with me?"

Jory nodded. "Yes."

Dax put his arms around him and hugged him. "Good, let's go do the paperwork."

CHAPTER FIVE

"How many months?" Freda asked Dax on the other end of the line.

"Three or four, maybe longer," Dax said. "Then he'll transfer to LA and go home to Ben."

"When does the broken heart come into it?" Freda asked.

"No broken heart. Stop that." He swallowed.

"I don't see what you're getting out of this. The program makes us say sorry to people we have wronged but we don't need to give them our whole life. Had reunion sex yet?"

"No. And that's not going to happen."

"Don't be so sure. At least you'd get some payback." She snorted.

"I don't need payback. I need to do this."

"Maybe he'll come to his senses and realize what he's missing."

"Can we change the subject? So, how's it going?"

"Everyone misses you, darling, especially me. I miss my best friend. Call me soon."

"Will do," Dax said and hung up.

"Tell me about him," Jory said. He'd obviously been eavesdropping on Dax's telephone call.

"It's a her."

"Oh, right, sorry. She was a he before?"

"Yes. Her family disowned her after the sex change. I love Freda. She's got a heart of gold. We're good friends," Dax said.

"What do you do at the club?" Jory asked. He was eating

breakfast at the counter, ready to start his second week of treatment. "Dance naked around poles?" He chuckled.

"Right." Dax nodded. "For sure. That's me."

"So, what?" Jory laughed.

"Everything. It's a dance club, very popular. Sometimes we have live bands. People drink and dance and have fun."

"Isn't it a weird choice for you, given that you and Freda are both addicts?"

"Maybe. But it doesn't bother me anymore. I don't bartend, Freda neither." Dax bit into some toast.

"Good. Do you play there, play guitar?"

"Sometimes. When we have a live band, they may invite me to play with them."

"I'm glad. You should never stop playing. You are the best there is, Dax," Jory told him.

"What is this all about?" He grinned. "What do you want now?"

"Nothing," Jory replied. "Can't I give you a compliment?"

"Thank you." Dax cleaned up his plate. "Ready? Let's go."

Sometimes the sessions went well. Other times, not so good. Dax went into the sessions only when Jory wanted him, too. Lately, he'd been telling Dax to wait outside.

One day, while Dax was waiting, Jory came running out of the room, rushing by him like a cyclone.

Dax jumped up and ran after him. It was raining. Jory kept running until finally, Dax caught up. "Whoa, whoa," Dax said, grabbing his arm. "What's going on?"

Jory kept his face turned away.

"Tell me," Dax urged.

"It's just that the therapist made me relive something I didn't want to," he told him, pulling away. "He says I have to deal with it. I told him to fuck himself."

Dax laughed. "They're used to that."

Jory looked at Dax. "He can't make me talk about something I don't want to. He wants every detail. How did I feel? I don't want to feel that ever again. Let's go home."

Dax stayed quiet for a long time in the car. As he pulled into the driveway, he looked at Jory. "When I was in therapy," Dax said, "I realized that I had repressed a lot of things."

Jory sighed. Jory glanced at him, but he didn't say anything.

Dax prepared what he would say next. "I never felt closer to anyone than I did to you, Jory. And still, in spite of that, during those years we were together, there were things I never told you."

Jory met his gaze. "Like what?"

"Like how I felt when my mother left. My father died, and instead of keeping me with her, she sent me to live with her brother and his wife. My uncle was great, but Aunt Grace didn't really want me there. Couldn't blame her. I was just dumped on her."

"When I met them at the wedding, they seemed so devoted to you," Rory said.

"When I got famous, my aunt was suddenly proud she'd raised me. At least that's what she told the tabloids. Made some money off it, too. She never really cared for me. She used to tell me often when Uncle Allan wasn't around."

"I'm so sorry," Rory said. "That must have really hurt. Why didn't your mother keep you after your dad died, Dax?" Rory asked.

"She was messed up, I guess."

Rory grabbed his hand. "I never did meet her. You invited her to the wedding, didn't you?"

Dax shook his head. "I don't know where she is," he said. "When the therapist in rehab made me talk about all that, I was so angry. I quit rehab, went on a bender for three days."

"Oh, no."

He nodded. "Freda found me in some sleazy place and dragged my ass back." He smiled. "She can be persuasive."

"I love her already," Rory said.

"So, are you going to tell me what you don't want to talk about?" Dax waited.

Rory opened the car door. "No," he said and got out.

Dax watched Rory walk into the house. He knew it wasn't easy. Therapy made you look yourself in the mirror with all the ghosts of your past standing in that mirror with you. A lot of people couldn't handle fame, not the kind of fame he'd had where you felt owned by the public. But deep down, he'd always felt abandoned, unloved. Maybe that was why he craved the attention, the adoration of millions. Then when he had it, he'd had no idea what to do with it.

When he was in therapy, he'd be asked when he felt happiness in his life. And it always came back to Jory. Jory loved him, that he knew, not because he was Dax Franklin, the rock star, but because he was just a man. His one regret was that he'd thrown it all away.

When he got out of the car, Susan was at the door. She looked frantic. "Dax, please, it's Jory. I think he's lost control."

Dax hurried into the house. There was banging and yelling coming from upstairs.

"I'm scared. I didn't dare go up there with him in this state."

"Stay here," he told her. "I'll take care of it. Go for a walk." He squeezed her shoulder. "It will be all right." Dax walked up the stairs. When he got to the top, he took a breath. He stood outside the door listening to Jory yelling, swearing. He waited. After a few minutes, it was quiet.

"Hey," Dax said. "You okay?"

"No."

"Can I come in?"

"Doors unlocked."

63

Dax walked into the room and closed the door behind him. Jory was sitting in the middle of the floor. Around him were pieces of ripped up posters. The lamp was on the floor, broken in two, and the night table had been overturned. There wasn't anything left on his bureau either.

Dax stepped over the lamp and sunk to the floor beside him, resting his back against the bottom of the bed. He didn't say anything for a little while.

There were tears drying on Jory's face.

Dax picked up a piece of poster. It was part of his hand and guitar. He put it back down again. "So, it was about me."

Jory glanced at him, then at the ripped pieces of glossy poster scattered around the floor. "What have I done? I love those posters." He started gathering the pieces as if he would try to piece them together.

Dax reached out for his arm, pulled him back. "Stop. It's done," he said, meeting his gaze. "We can't glue them back together."

Jory made a sound in his throat. It sounded like a sob.

"The past is gone," Dax said. "All we have is now. You need to get well. You need to deal with whatever it is you've been holding inside."

Jory got to his feet. He turned and looked down at Dax sitting there.

"If you want to hit me, go ahead, if you want to call me every rotten name in the book, that's okay, too," Dax said. "It doesn't matter how you feel about me, Jory, as long as it helps you to heal."

Jory stayed silent, walking over to the window.

"You told me in the hospital that you hated me. Do you remember?" Dax stood, too. He kept his distance.

Jory nodded silently, not looking at him.

"It's okay," he said.

Jory turned and looked at him. "If only I could mean that."

He pointed at him. "You, from the moment you came into my life, you turned it upside down. There was no way I ever wanted to live without you. I needed you more than you ever needed me, loved you more than you loved me."

"That's not true," Dax protested.

Jory walked over to him. "Do you know why I know it's true? It's because you left me. You had the strength to walk away, to conceive of a world, a life, without me." Jory's words were now choked with tears. "I could have never walked away from you. And I can't tell that therapist what happened to me when I came back to the hospital and found you gone."

Dax placed both hands on Jory's shoulders. He held back his own grief, but he was trembling deep inside. "Don't tell him then, tell me instead."

Jory backed away. "Why?" he scoffed. "So, you can find out how weak I am?"

"You need to trust me, Rory, trust that I care enough about you to acknowledge and respect those feelings. I know you loved me."

Jory looked at the carpet.

"I felt it every time you touched me, every time you said my name. In fact, no one had ever loved me like that before."

Rory let out a cry. "And yet, you left me!" Rory went to his knees, sobbing. "You just left me," he cried. "Without a good-bye. I didn't know where you were, if you were all right. I thought you'd come back. And you didn't."

Dax went down to the floor with him. He tried to embrace him, but Rory pushed him off.

"No. Don't. Please, don't touch me."

"Tell me, Jory," Dax insisted, "and I'll tell you what it was like for me. Okay?" He met Jory's eyes.

Jory let out a yell. "I need a drink so badly."

Dax didn't want to admit that this was the first time in a long while, he, too, felt the urge to drink. "It will pass. Talk to me."

Jory reached out and touched Dax's arm. "I will. I promise. I'm just not ready. Okay?" He got to his feet. "I'm so tired, Dax."

Dax stood, too. "I'll leave you to rest. When you're ready, we'll talk, really talk, okay?" He glanced at Jory over his shoulder.

Jory attempted a smile. "Thanks. If I haven't told you how much it means to me that you are—"

Dax put up a hand. "No need." He walked out and closed the door.

Too many emotions, too much grief, Dax needed some air.

Susan was downstairs. She hadn't gone out. She looked at Dax's face when he came down the stairs and came over to hug him. "Oh, honey, are you all right?"

Dax nodded. "Thanks," he said. "You know, Susan, you're the closest I've ever come to having a mother."

She hugged him again. "I'm always here for you, Dax, even when, if, you and Jory are not together. You know?"

"Yes, I know. Listen, I'm going for a walk."

"Do you want me to come with you?" Susan asked.

"No, if you don't mind, I need some time alone."

When he got outside, he pulled up the collar of his coat. It was spring but it was hard to tell. The wind was brisk, and it hit him hard in the face as if punishing him for his sins. He began to walk faster, tears stinging his eyes. He told himself it was the cold, but he knew better.

He passed a church, a school, walked across the intersection. He wasn't sure where he was going. There was a little strip mall in the distance, a coffee place, a small market, and a liquor store. When he got to the Mall, he walked into the parking lot. There was a bench there. He sat, watching the people walk in and out of the liquor store. It would be so easy, wouldn't it, to drink this pain away, to wipe out three years of sobriety.

He took out his cell phone. He called Freda. He got her answering machine. He hung up. He could hear the glass bottles bumping up against each other in the brown paper bags as one customer, and then another went back to their cars.

He closed his eyes, remembering that evening.

After Rory had left him in the hospital, he'd felt optimistic. Jory made him believe that it was going to be all right. They'd be together, and there would be sacrifices, no more two-year tours and partying all night. They had each other. He was going conquer this, make up for everything, be the best husband to Jory he could. Nothing else mattered but their love.

He was almost asleep when Ben walked in, like a vampire in the night coming to steal your life away. It started out okay. Ben seemed concerned. "The band will get a replacement until you're out of rehab, Dax," Ben said. "The fans will not be happy, but they'll adjust." He came closer. "They will forget your name soon enough."

Dax said nothing. That was cruel, but he didn't expect Ben to be thrilled about the rehab.

"You're a coward, and you have no self-control, Dax," Ben said suddenly. "You've let everyone down, the guys in the band, me, and especially Jory."

"I'm going to make it up to him," Dax said.

"Ha, do you think Jory, now at the threshold of his career, is going to want his name mixed up with some washed up, drugged out, has been?"

Ben had a point.

"Do you love him, Dax?" Ben demanded.

"Of course. Why do you think I'm going to rehab?"

"Because you are a coward, afraid to end up like your father."

"You bastard," Dax told him.

"Die young, leave a good-looking corpse, kid." Ben grinned. He leaned in closer. "I don't give a shit if you rot in rehab, Dax, but if you love Jory like you say, you'll do the decent thing and leave him.

If you stay, he'll give up everything for you because he's in love with the idea of you, but that's over now. Look at you."

When Ben left, his words echoed through his mind. He couldn't deny it. He was no good for Jory. Jory was getting popular, developing a fan-base. Jory would find love again. He'd be all right, so much better off without him.

He'd left in the middle of the night, found his clothes, and just walked out of the hospital. He was in pain, he was completely devastated, and what he really wanted was to drown in the bottle. He called his driver. They stopped at the liquor store and he drank until he passed out. When he was sober enough the next day, he took a taxi to the airport.

He was leaving, going anywhere. Vancouver, Canada had just been a place up on the departure board. He knew no one there. That was good. He booked the flight, threw up several times in the washroom, and tossed his cell phone in the garbage can. He passed out a few minutes after he was seated on the plane.

After he'd arrived, he found a hotel room and kept on drinking. He didn't care if he died or not. He didn't want to live without Jory. He woke up in the psychiatric wing of a hospital. He'd had a seizure. Freda was in the same wing. She, too, a chronic alcoholic. Dax knew that he and Freda had given each other a reason to live. Misery loves company, as the saying goes.

How could he tell Jory that? But he would. It was time. Just like it was time that Jory told him what he'd been keeping inside for so long, what was causing him the deepest pain.

Dax stood, staring at the liquor store for a few more minutes. He saw the face of the doctor in Vancouver, heard those words.

Mr. Franklin, you've been lucky. But you can never drink again. Next time, it could kill you.

"Dax!"

Someone called out his name. He turned around to see Jory running across the street.

"Dax, oh thank God, are you all right?" Jory was breathing hard. His gaze strayed to the liquor store and then back to Dax.

"I wasn't going to," Dax said, shaking his head. But there was some doubt in his mind.

Jory came over and hugged him, then released him. "Come on." Jory took his arm. "Let's go home."

As they walked, Dax began to talk. He told him everything, what he'd done when he left the hospital and how he ended up in Vancouver.

Jory remained quiet, listening as Dax talked. They stopped on the corner. Jory looked at him, his eyes filled with tears. "You said Ben came to the hospital. I want to know exactly what he said that night."

"No," Dax replied. They started to walk again. "I already told you that some of what he said rang true. I didn't want you to put your career on hold for me, to be a pity case."

Jory grabbed his arm. "You listen to me. You were never a pity case. You were my life." Tears rolled down his face. "When I told you that you were more important than anything else in my life, I meant it."

"I know, but you shouldn't have had to make that choice, Jory." Dax reached over and wiped Jory's tears. "I chose to drink. I chose to destroy my career. Not you."

"Why won't you tell me what he said to you?" Jory persisted after a few minutes.

"Because," Dax replied, "I promised myself I wouldn't come between you and Ben, no matter what. You chose Ben. Obviously, you must—" He couldn't say love. He began again. " . . . want to be with him."

"I owe him," Jory said softly.

Dax narrowed his eyes. "What?"

Jory took his hand. They were standing near some trees. The wind had died down some, but it was still cold. "When I

came to the hospital that day and you were gone, I lost it."
Jory shook his head. "I was frantic. I thought you'd died, or, I
didn't know what to think. You left without anyone seeing
you. None of the staff knew. I called your cell phone over and
over, left a hundred messages. So, I sat in your empty hospital
room for a long time, until someone came and told me I had
to leave."

Dax nodded, feeling Jory's pain as he spoke.

"When I left the hospital, I knew you'd gone, and I also
suspected you weren't coming back. I assumed I'd get a call
telling me they'd found you in some ditch somewhere, you
were dead, or—" He swallowed.

"You don't have to," Dax said softly.

He nodded, clutching his arm. "Yes, I do. I have to tell you.
You deserve to know. I found a room in the scuzziest place in
town. I drank a lot. I went out and found a gay bar. I bought
some drugs, took those, too. And in the dark, I was sure I'd
found you."

"What do you mean?"

"He was for hire, a male prostitute, and God, in the dark,
he made me think of you, same height, same built, dark hair.
He had more drugs. I gave him a ton of money and brought
him back to the hotel. In the dark, you'd come back to me."

"Oh, Jory," Dax whispered.

"I kept drinking and fucking. He had some other drugs.
We took those, too. The problem was when the sun came up."

Dax closed his eyes. "What happened?"

"He reached for me. I saw your face morph into his. You
weren't there. I knew it. I had to face it. Something wasn't
right with me. I was really fucked up. The drugs, the booze. I
started hitting him. I lashed out, accusing him of tricking me.
I might have called him Dax. I couldn't stop hitting him. There
was blood everywhere."

"Oh, my God. You didn't kill him, did you?" Dax grabbed

his forearm.

"No, but I did a number on his face, broke his nose, split lip. He told me he wouldn't be able to work like that. I, too, was battered and bruised. That's when Ben called. I'd missed a rehearsal. He wanted to know where I was. The prostitute was in the bathroom, but he wasn't going to leave. He was ranting. "I know who you are. I'm going to the press. I'm going to tell them what you did."

"So, you told Ben?"

"He fixed everything. We gave that guy enough money to shut him up, made sure he had no pictures on his cell phone, which he did, of course. He had the room cleaned up, and he snuck me out of there." Jory met Dax's eyes. "Ben was all I had. I was fragile. I fell into a depression. I didn't want to get out of bed. A drink here or there and it helped. It got me on stage. It helped me sleep. I woke up every day wondering where you were, if you were all right. I know you don't know this, but I hired a detective to find you. I told him not to approach, just to report. Mom thought that when Ben and I announced we were a couple that lifted me out of the depression, but it was knowing you were alive, and okay that helped me to face each day again."

"Are you afraid to leave Ben? Are you afraid he will expose what happened?"

"No. I don't believe he'd do that. It would be as damaging to him as it would be to me."

"So, you do love Ben," Dax said. "You stay with him because you want to."

"It's complicated," Jory said. "I needed someone. He was there. Whether he manipulated the situation, or not, he was all I had because you'd abandoned me, Dax."

"It's my fault you're fucking Ben then?" Dax snapped. "You can blame me for a shitload of things, Jory, you in Ben's bed, that's all on you." He started to walk again.

71

Jory kept pace beside him without speaking. Before they turned the corner to the house, Jory put a hand on Dax's arm. "Would it have hurt you less if it had been someone else?"

Dax looked at him. "Yes," he said.

As they turned the corner, they saw a car in the driveway, parked beside Dax's rental. It was a black BMW.

"It's Ben," Jory announced without any discernable emotion.

"Great," Dax muttered. "Isn't this the cherry on the fucking cake?"

"I've been putting him off for weeks."

"Happy reunion," Dax told him. He turned around and headed off in the opposite direction. The last person he wanted to see right now was Ben Lennox. He checked the time. It was well past supper time, and he was getting hungry. He'd find a place to eat, take some time to be by himself, digest everything Jory had told him.

He was glad Jory had gotten that off his chest. Hopefully, he could talk about it in Group. It had been a while since he'd spoken to his sponsor. Given the events today, perhaps it was time, or maybe he could find an AA meeting somewhere, just sit in. Right now, he'd eat, call Freda. That would help.

He opted for a small family restaurant. It was mostly empty. The waiter was a young guy, handsome. He gave Dax the menu and walked away. Dax couldn't help but admire the way he looked in those tight, black pants. God, it had been awhile.

He ordered a steak, coffee, house salad, and checked his messages. He had a dozen or more from Freda, pictures, some friends in Vancouver telling him to come home.

He skipped dessert, ordered more coffee, and got Freda on the phone. He realized he'd been here over two hours. There were no more customers. They were probably waiting for him to leave.

He didn't tell Freda about wanting to drink. She'd worry. She'd most likely hop on a plane and come down here to beat the crap out of him. He'd been away almost two months now. The worst was yet to come. It got harder nearer the end, scarier when you knew one day you'd be out of treatment.

He finished his coffee. The waiter came over to the table and to Dax's surprise, sat down opposite him. "Hi."

"Hi," Dax said.

"I'm sorry but are you, Dax Franklin?"

Dax nodded.

"Oh, my God," he said, smiling. "I saw you play in one of your last shows right here at the arena. The guitarist they have now, Hank Munroe, you can play rings around him. God, I don't even listen to Intoxication any more. You were the heartbeat of that band."

"Thank you," Dax said.

"What are you doing now? You must play somewhere?"

"I'm mostly out of business," Dax said with a smile.

"I recognized you right away, even with the beard," he said. "You're so gorgeous. Ah, we're closing. You want to get a drink?"

"I don't drink," Dax said, meeting his gaze. "But thanks. I'm flattered."

He leaned across the table. "We don't have to drink. We can go to my place."

Dax just looked at him.

"If I'm out of line, tell me, I just thought the way you were looking at me that . . ." He trailed off.

"No, no, it's okay. I was looking," Dax said with a smile. "Unfortunately" — he held up his left hand — "I'm married."

"Jory Carter, right?"

"Um."

"He's really sweet, good singer but he's living with his manager, isn't he?"

The question hung in the air between them. Yes. Jory was living with his manager. So, what was holding him back? This guy was cute, and he wanted to spend some time with him. Jory was with Ben right now. Would it be wrong?

Dax put some money on the table with a generous tip, then stood. "Sorry," he said, "I can't."

Chapter Six

His mother wasn't happy that Ben was there, but she had too much class to make a scene. She made supper and small talk. She took Jory aside to ask him where Dax was.

"I guess he wanted some time alone," Jory said. He was a little worried.

"He didn't want to see Ben," Susan added.

"Probably. Do you mind if he stays the night or we can stay in a hotel?"

"You are not going anywhere with Ben right now, Jory. He can stay but please don't throw this in Dax's face."

"Maybe Dax won't come home tonight," Jory said. "Come on. Let's have coffee in the living room. I'll make it."

When they were settled with their coffee, Ben talked about the sales of Jory's latest CD.

"That's great, right, Mom?" Jory said. He felt uncomfortable knowing how his mother felt about Ben.

"Super," she said, "but there are more important things right now."

"Just because Jory is in rehab doesn't mean we want his career to falter, Susan," Ben said. "I've been keeping everything chugging along, holding off the press, who want to know where Jory is. Franklin hasn't been talking to the press, has he?"

"If you mean, Dax," his mother said, "no. I don't think he's much of a fan of the press. Anyway, he'd never exploit Jory." She looked right at him.

Jory cleared his throat. "You are staying the night, right,

Ben?"

"I could book us a luxury room." Ben reached over and took Jory's hand.

"You can stay with Jory in his room," his mom said, getting to her feet. "Jory needs to be here just in case. If you'll excuse me, I'm going to get some towels and such. Then I think I'll go to bed. I'm tired."

"Thank you, Susan, for your hospitality," Ben told her.

She gave him a polite smile and left the room.

Jory breathed an inward sigh of relief.

Ben leaned over and kissed him. "It's been a while since I slept in your bed upstairs."

"Ben, you have never slept with me in that bed. We always rented a room."

"Oh, okay," he said. "It's an adventure."

"You know you haven't asked me about rehab once since you got here," Jory told him.

"I didn't think you wanted to talk about that. I mean, that Dax mess."

"Dax mess?"

"Well, it's all about him, right? You work through how badly he treated you, get control, get a damn divorce, and marry me."

"This isn't about Dax treating me badly. He never treated me badly. He abandoned me, left me, and made me feel as if the bottom had dropped out of my world, but he never mistreated me."

"Any way you choose to think about Dax is fine, Jory, if it makes you feel better and gets you back on stage."

Jory narrowed his eyes. "You think I don't know what I feel?"

"I think you romanticize your time with Dax, that's all."

"Romanticize? Isn't that another word for making shit up?

Do you think I made up my feelings for Dax? Maybe our marriage isn't real, either? Maybe I made that up, too?"

"Why are you angry? I don't understand."

Jory paced a little, and then he stopped. "The problem isn't Dax. The problem is fame, crowds, press, and fans. It's not a normal life."

"It's the life many people dream about but never get to live, Jory," Ben protested.

"But what if my dream was to be with Dax? What if he was what made me happy? What if he was enough all along, and the rest of this is what's make-believe?"

"That's bullshit. He was a wreck before he left. He did you a favor, leaving."

"Yeah, and he had some help making that decision, didn't he?" Jory looked at him.

"What do you mean? What has he told you?"

"Nothing. He won't. But I know you went to see him, and you convinced him to leave, that it was better for me."

"Well, damn it, it was. And you know it. Listen, Jory, I think you need to come home to LA. This treatment is messing with your head. Let's drop it, okay? I've come all this way to see you. I miss you. Let's go upstairs and I'll show you how much, okay?"

Jory looked at him. "I've really got a headache. Do you mind if we don't do this? You can have my room. I'll sleep downstairs on the sofa."

"Jory?" Ben walked over to him.

"It's the treatment. I need space. It will get better. I'm sorry, Ben, just for tonight, okay?"

"Okay. I'll go on upstairs."

Jory watched him leave the living room. He sank onto the sofa. He leaned back and closed his eyes. *Dax.* He remembered, shortly after they'd married that they'd rented a cabin in the woods, somewhere quiet where Dax could escape the public eye. They swam in the lake, cooked on the barbeque, laughed, talked, and made love. Jory couldn't get enough of touching him, looking at him, watching him while he slept. They were so happy. Jory fell asleep every night in his arms, and for almost a week, it was only them. Jory could have stayed there with Dax the rest of their lives. Then, one morning, they heard the helicopters overhead. The press had found them. It was over. *Dax. I love you.* That had never changed, and it never would.

When he opened his eyes again, it was Dax who was looking down at him, covering him over with a blanket. "Hey," Dax said, "what are you doing down here? Where's Ben?"

"I had a headache. Where did you go?" Jory sat up. "I was worried."

"Were you waiting up for me, like an overprotective father?" Dax laughed.

"Stop it, Dax," Jory snapped. "Seriously, where were you?"

"Whoa? What's this now?" Dax narrowed his eyes. "I don't think you have earned the right to give me the third degree."

"I'm sorry. You're right," Jory said. "I have no right."

Dax sat down beside him on the sofa. "If you must know, I went to eat a steak. I called Freda. A waiter recognized me and tried to take me home. I said no. That's about it."

Jory looked at him. "He wasn't your type?"

Dax shrugged. "He'd be anyone's type. He was cute but I'd drunk too much coffee."

Jory looked at him, then laughed. "Right. Good reason."

"He was great for my ego, that's about it. So, what did Ben say?"

"He thinks you're a fantasy."

"Oh, I don't even want to go there. I'm not his fantasy, I hope." Dax made a funny face.

"No, mine. And that's the problem. None of what we had was real." Jory looked at him. Their shoulders were touching.

God, he was so close, too close.

"Ouch, okay. You believe that?"

"No, I don't," Jory said. "I told him everything else about us, the fame, our careers, that is the fantasy."

Dax tilted his head. "How did you get so smart?"

Jory laughed. "I don't feel smart, baby."

Dax leaned in and pressed his lips against Jory's forehead. He went to get up. Jory held onto his arm. Dax looked at him. "What? Jory?"

"Kiss me," he whispered. "Don't ask why, don't question it, but right now, I might die if you don't kiss me."

Dax lowered his head and pressed his mouth to Jory's. Jory breathed in his kiss like oxygen. Dax withdrew. Jory licked his lips, sucking on the bottom one to keep the taste of him. It wasn't long enough. He wanted his mouth to stay there. "I want you. You know that, don't you?"

Dax got to his feet. "Yes, I know."

"And you want me still? Say you do, Dax." Jory stood. He waited, looking at him.

"Ben is upstairs," Dax reminded him, looking at the ceiling.

"I know that. You didn't answer my question, Dax. Do you still want me?" Jory insisted.

Dax moved his face close to his and rubbed his nose with his then gave it a quick kiss. "Do you have to ask? Goodnight, Jory."

Jory watched him walk out of the room. He was trembling inside. Could they make this work? Could all this be leading him back to Dax, to the man he loved? He hadn't thought about his career once since he'd been home. He hadn't thought about Ben either. He wanted to get well, and he wanted Dax.

All these thoughts were running through his mind when he heard some sort of commotion coming from under him. Jory took the stairs to the basement where Dax slept in the guest room. He heard two voices as he got closer. It was Ben and Dax. Oh no.

"You need to convince him to come back to LA," Ben insisted.

"I'm not going to convince Jory of anything," Dax said. "And that would be a mistake. Listen, don't talk to me about this. Talk to Jory. If Jory wants to continue rehab out there, he will."

"Not with you filling his head with nonsense," Ben accused.

"I don't fill his head with anything," Dax retorted.

"Or his bed? You must be getting it somewhere, and from what I remember, you used to have a lineup. You must have been pretty good."

"A shame you never got to find out, you pervert," Dax threw back.

Jory chose that moment to come into the room. "I don't want to hear any more of this. Ben, what are you doing down here?"

"Talking to your husband," he sneered. "You need to come home."

"I am home," Jory replied. "And you need to leave."

"What?" Ben looked confused. Dax left the room.

"You heard me. Go home, Ben. Go back to LA. I'm going to finish the treatment program here. Dax is helping me through this. He doesn't think I make up my feelings. He cares."

"He just wants a quick fuck, that's all," Ben said. "You'd throw everything away for a night in bed with him?"

Jory smiled. "Yeah, I think I would. So, go stay in that luxury room you wanted."

"Are you saying it's over between us, after all I've done for you?"

"Covering up my addiction wasn't doing me any favors,

Ben, but it was filling your pockets. You never loved me. Maybe you're the one that lives in a fantasy."

Ben just stared at him. "You'll regret this." Ben pointed at him.

"You know I regret many things in my life, but some-how" — Jory smiled — "I doubt very much, this will be one of them. Goodbye, Ben." Jory walked upstairs.

Dax was standing in the kitchen. "You okay?"

"I am now," he said, reaching out his hand. "Come with me upstairs."

Dax squeezed his hand, but he shook his head. "No. I don't want to be your rebound tonight, Jory. Take some time."

Jory let go of his hand. "Okay, you're right as usual."

Dax smiled. "Doesn't mean that was easy for me, you know?"

"I know, but like you say, self-control, right?" They heard the door slam shut in the living room, a car engine start. A tear ran down Jory's face.

Dax pulled him into his arms and held him. "It's okay."

"Why am I crying? I did the right thing. I shouldn't be cry-ing?" Jory told him.

Dax held him away from him and smiled. "I'd find it strange if you didn't shed a tear or two, Jory. You just ended a relationship."

"Why in the hell are you so wonderful?" Jory stroked his hair.

Dax laughed. "Go to bed, Jory."

Jory stole a quick kiss. "I will. I'm sure the tears will be dry tomorrow."

Dax nodded with a wink.

By the time Jory had crawled into bed, there were no more tears over Ben, but he was worried. What would happen now with his record sales and concert dates? Would he be sued? And even if he'd broken up with Ben romantically, he was still his manager.

His thoughts turned to Dax. He really needed him tonight. He wanted to hold him and make love to him again. The last time they'd made love was over three years ago. It was still etched in his memory. Dax thought by denying him he was doing what was required in the situation they were in. But, damn it, what in the hell did that mean? If Dax could hold back like that maybe he was over him, didn't want him as much as Jory did him.

Jory couldn't sleep. He turned on his cell phone. There were several messages from Ben.

We need to talk. I'm sure you didn't mean what you said. I should have been more compassionate. It's true. I'm jealous. Dax is at your side and I'm busy running your career. Don't throw it all away. I'm sorry. Please, let's talk.

Jory let out a yell and hurled his phone across the room. He got out of bed and went downstairs. It was after two in the morning. When he walked into the den, he noticed the television was on. Dax was awake, watching videos on YouTube, volume turned low.

"What are you doing awake?" Dax asked when Jory walked in.

"I could ask you the same thing." Jory came over and sat on the end of the pull-out sofa. He looked at the television. "That's Intoxication."

Dax sat upright in bed. "Yeah, their latest concert in Toronto."

"Luke has really aged," Jory said. "And that's not Hank Monroe playing lead guitar. Who's that?"

"Hank quit. I don't know why. They replaced him with Doug Lalonde."

"What do you think?"

"He's not a great improviser but he's a better fit. Luke didn't encourage much deviation on stage." Dax glanced at him. "What's up? Why can't you sleep?"

Jory shrugged. "Can I just hang out here for a while?"

"Sure." Dax patted the space beside him, and Jory settled in next to him. "Can we watch some videos of Intoxication when you were with them?"

Dax passed him the remote control. "Watch what you want."

Jory found the video's where Dax was singing. He sang along, feeling relaxed now. Dax was so close and yet so far. He wanted to touch him, but he didn't want to ruin the moment. "You looked so sexy," he said, glancing at him. "You were happy when you were performing."

"Yes, I guess I was. It was when I was off stage that I wasn't."

"Those girls are going crazy in the front." Jory laughed. "I can't blame them."

Dax gave him a playful push. "Shut-up."

"Luke wanted to be the sex symbol of the group, but it was really you," Jory told him. "Luke was always jealous of that. I remember how he was sometimes when I'd go on tour with you. Do you ever hear from any of the guys in the band?"

"Reggie sends me messages and texts."

"He was a great drummer, a nice guy."

"Yeah, he's been having a lot of health problems. I think he's on dialysis."

"Oh, no. Sorry to hear that. He could really drink, that guy," Jory murmured.

"We all could."

Jory put his head on Dax's shoulder. "Can I sleep here?"

"Jory, I really don't think that—" Dax began.

Jory met his gaze. "Do you have to think all the time? I meant just to sleep."

Dax reached over to stroke his hair. "Jory, baby, if you stay here with me tonight, we are going to do a hell of a lot more than sleep."

Jory smiled. "So, you do still want me?"

"God damn it, Jory." Dax pulled the covers off and put his feet on the floor.

Jory moved over and slid his hands up over Dax's back. "I love this tattoo of the guitar," he said, pressing his lips to Dax's left shoulder. The guitar was wrapped in musical notes and red roses. He moved his lips from Dax's shoulder to the back of his neck, crawled closer to him so he could wrap his arms around his waist.

Dax let his head go back a minute and Jory turned his head so that he could press his mouth to his. They kissed. Um. It was sweet and cautious, and Jory wanted more. He ran a hand over Dax's hair and pulled a little, keeping Dax's head turned so the kiss could continue, getting deeper and more insistent as it continued. Jory's arms tightened around his back, one hand moving down to slid into the waistband of Dax's pajama pants.

"You never used to wear anything to bed," Jory breathed against Dax's throat as his fingers moved lightly over the length of Dax's cock.

"Your mom," he replied, his voice shaking.

"My mom would love it. You're so damn beautiful." He wrapped his fist around Dax's hard cock. "And big."

Dax made a soft sound in his throat. Jory backed off. He took off his bathrobe but left his underwear. He pulled Dax down onto his back. He took his time looking at him. "I've missed you so much," he said softly, not giving Dax a chance to protest. He left the bed and got on his knees. He spread Dax's thighs.

"Let's get rid of these things," Jory breathed, pulling off the pajama pants. Jory slid his palms up over Dax's thighs, then lowered his mouth to his cock. He tasted the pre-cum there and inhaled his scent. Dax's body had always been incredible, well-muscled and lean, and although he thought he'd never say this, Dax was even more beautiful than he had been three years ago.

Jory licked up his shaft and felt Dax's hand in his hair, at first, lightly, then with more pressure as he pressed Jory's head down with more force. "Swallow it," he urged. "Yeah, come on, come on. Fuck, fuck."

Jory took more and more of Dax's cock into his mouth, and tilting his head, he had enough leverage to take his cock even deeper into his throat. He'd gotten in a lot of practice with Dax. He had this thing about not going all the way until he found his one and only. He made Dax wait until they got married. Poor Dax. Anyway, Jory became quite the expert.

When he tasted Dax in his mouth, he backed away, wiping at his lips. He wanted to keep the taste of him. Dax sat up. He pulled Jory to his feet. He smiled at him and kissed him again, his hands moving over Jory's body, pushing off the underwear as he cupped his ass cheeks.

Dax's mouth moved to Jory's chest, tonguing his nipples, then dropping to his knees. Dax stroked Jory's erection and took his balls into his mouth. Jory dug his fingernails into Dax's scalp. "Oh, shitttt. Stop, Dax. Stop."

Dax looked up at him.

"I don't want to come. I want you inside me. You got condoms, lube, anything?"

Dax laughed. He stood. "Yeah."

Jory clung to him, kissing his skin, tracing the letters of his name on his chest. "I love you. You know. I fucking love you, Dax. I never stopped."

"Shush," he said, opening a small accessory bag he kept in the side table. He took out lube and condoms.

Jory took the condoms. "Come here," he urged. "I want to put it on. I want you now. Come on."

Dax touched his hair. "Breathe, baby. Breathe." Dax squeezed some lube onto his fingers. He pressed Jory down onto the bed. "Raise your knees." He took two cushions and placed them under Jory's hips. "I want to look at you when you come. And you're going to come," he told him.

"I'm coming now just looking at you." Jory was still trying to rip open the condom package.

Dax crawled onto the bed and leaned down over Jory. They kissed. Jory ran one of his hands over his back, his round, delicious ass. As they were kissing, Jory felt one lubed finger push up inside of him.

Jory made a sound of pleasure in his throat. Two fingers, then three began thrusting, and Jory's head went back into the pillow. "Oh yeah," he said softly. "Yeah."

Dax pulled out his fingers and took the condom from Jory. He undid the package and moved up closer. Jory took the condom back and unrolled it onto Dax's cock. Dax leaned down and kissed him again. "Are you sure?" he asked Jory.

"Yes, yes," Jory urged.

Dax lifted Jory's legs onto his shoulders. When he felt the head of Dax's cock push up inside of him, tears filled his eyes. He started sobbing.

Dax stopped in mid thrust. "I'm hurting you," he said.

"No, no." Jory reached up and touched his face. "I just missed you so much. Don't stop, baby, don't stop."

A half hour later, they lay there, side by side. Jory felt a peace like he hadn't in a long time. He took Dax's hand in his. Dax hadn't said anything since he'd come inside him. It had started easy and gentle and ended in that mad, crazy sex that Jory remembered from long ago. He was sure his mother had heard them, but he knew she'd be happy. She loved Dax.

Finally, Jory broke the silence. "Are you okay? Are we okay?"

Dax turned his head and looked at him. "I don't know."

Jory moved closer, kissed his shoulder, and then put his head there. "Are you sorry?"

"How can I be? I let it happen. I was powerless to stop it."

Jory bit his bottom lip. "I know you said you didn't want to be rebound for Ben, but you weren't."

"I kind of was," he said. "You felt alone. I was convenient."

"Seriously? You think that you could have been any guy?" Jory sighed.

"Not any guy but . . . I don't know, Jory. My head is spinning. Okay?" He moved away, put his feet on the floor. "You just broke up with Ben. He's still your manager. You could get back together. After this is over, you have a career to go back to, and I have a life somewhere else." Dax looked at him. "Maybe our time was the past, and it's over."

"I can't believe it. I thought you still loved me."

"I do," Dax said. "I told you that will never change, but that doesn't mean we can go back. This is what I didn't want. You don't need this drama during treatment. I shouldn't have lost control. You were the vulnerable one, not me."

"You're just like Ben," he accused, getting out of bed. He put on his robe. "You keep telling me what I feel or don't feel."

"I didn't tell you anything. I'm concerned that this is a lot for you to handle right now, that's all. And you know what?"

Dax was facing him.

"What?" Jory demanded.

"This is a lot for me, too. I wanted to drink today. I have been texting with my sponsor."

"Maybe you should go home, and I'll do this by myself." Jory turned to go.

Dax took his arm and swung him around. "Listen to me. I signed on to this, and I will see it through until the end, no matter what happens, okay?"

Jory swallowed.

Dax lifted his chin and looked him in the eye. "Okay?"

Jory nodded. "What's going to happen to us?"

"I don't know. I know only one thing, once you get through the treatment and you feel strong again, you'll be prepared to make some decisions."

"And you, what if I decide that what I want is you." Jory waited for an answer.

"I can't go back to that life, Jory. I won't. So, again, it's your career or me. And I never wanted you to make that choice."

"But I will, okay?" Jory reached out and caressed his cheek. "I'll do it with my heart, and I won't look back again."

"Fair enough," Dax said. "But it's not the time."

Jory left Dax and went back to his room. He lay in bed with his eyes opened, waiting for the morning to come.

He must have dozed off because when he opened his eyes again, the sun was up. He looked around for his phone. He found it on the floor in the corner. More messages from Ben?

This time it was a different kind of message.

Jory, great news, you've been nominated for an award for your latest CD. Call me. Ben xxx

It was exciting. Jory pressed speed dial for Ben. He knew it was early in LA, just after four in the morning.

Ben was awake, probably back from some all-night party. "Jory, baby, you get the news?"

"This is so . . . unexpected. Wow. Is it real, Ben?"

"Yes. And you're going to win. We have a lot to do, talk shows and press conferences. Baby, you are going to need to finish your treatments here. And I'll agree to be more sensitive and less of an asshole. We could go to couples counseling."

Jory tensed. "Ben, we need a break from each other for a while, okay? Rent me a place, a condo near the studio."

"Of course. Okay, we'll take it slow. When can you be here?"

"I'll talk to them today about transferring me to an outpatient place there. I need to continue my treatment."

"Of course, and you will, baby. This is wonderful news."

"Yes," Jory said. "I'll call you as soon as I speak with my counselor today."

"I'm sorry about our fight."

"I know. Talk later." Jory hung up.

Jory went to take a shower. He got dressed, rehearsing how he was going to tell Dax. He knew he wouldn't be happy.

When he walked into the kitchen, his mother was making coffee. "Hello, baby," she said, kissing him on the top of the head. "Late night?" She grinned at him.

"Hope we didn't . . . where is Dax?" He looked around.

"He was in the shower downstairs. I heard the water running. He's out now."

"I have something to tell you," Jory said.

She beamed. "I think I know. You and Dax?"

"No, not that. Let's wait until Dax is here." Jory wasn't sure how he was going to say this.

When Dax came into the kitchen, his dark hair was still damp. He wore a pair of blue jeans and a navy shirt. It played up the blue of his eyes. He'd shaved some, his beard, closer to his jaw. If only he weren't so damn beautiful.

"Morning," Dax said.

"Good morning," his mother replied, pouring the coffee.

Jory met Dax's blue eyes.

Dax gave him a curious look as he slid onto a stool at the counter. "You all right?"

"I have some news," he said. "Mom, please sit down."

She took a seat. "What is it?"

"My CD, *Over My Shoulder*, has been nominated for CD of the year."

"That's wonderful news," his mom said, getting up to hug him.

Dax stayed silent, looking at him.

Jory glanced at him, waiting for a reaction.

"Good," Dax said. "It's a great CD. So, what else?"

"What do you mean?" Jory sipped his coffee.

"When are you leaving?" Dax asked.

"He's not," his mother said. "Not until treatment is over." She looked at him. "Right?"

"I'm going to transfer to LA."

"No," she said. "Dax, talk some sense into him, please."

Dax stood. He held up his hands and walked out of the kitchen.

"Damn it," Jory muttered under his breath. "Mom, listen, I need to be in LA now. I will have to make appearances, and my CD is — please try and understand. At least I broke up with Ben. I'll be living apart from him."

"And what about Dax?"

Jory stood. "Can't talk about that now, Mom. I have to get ready to go to the clinic. Maybe Dax won't want to — "

"Ready?" Dax asked, poking his head in the kitchen. "I'll wait in the car."

His mother looked at him. "Are you just going to pretend nothing happened last night?"

"Were you listening at the God damned door?" Jory snapped.

"No, I couldn't help but . . . Jory" — she grabbed his hand — "don't mess this up."

"Gotta' go, Mom, don't worry," he said, pecking her cheek.

The car was running when Jory came out. Dax was sitting in the driver's seat, his hands on the wheel.

When Jory closed the door and did up his belt, Dax pulled out of the driveway. He didn't say anything.

Jory was furiously texting the people he knew who were sending their congratulations. As they neared the clinic, he turned off his phone. "Too many," he said, smiling. He looked at Dax. They'd stopped for a light. "You going to say anything?"

"Nope," he said. "I know the power of that stuff."

"What?"

"I won countless guitar awards. The first one was pretty damn exciting."

"Then you understand why I have to be in LA," Jory told him.

Dax hit the gas. "I don't want to talk about this. You do what you have to do."

"You could come with me," Jory blurted.

"No, thanks."

They pulled into the parking lot. "Are you that afraid?"

Dax turned off the engine. "I'm not afraid. I'm just really over it." He opened the door and got out.

Jory followed him. "Come in with me today."

Dax raised an eyebrow. "Okay. Let's do it."

Jory had individual counseling before group today. He liked Harry, his counselor, despite what had happened last time. He hoped he'd get one just as good in LA. When they entered the office, Harry nodded to Dax. "Both of you today. Great."

CHAPTER SEVEN

Dax attempted to smile, but he wasn't feeling it. He'd keep his emotions to himself. This was Jory's time. This was the last place he wanted to be right now. He had the feeling that Jory was using him as a buffer. He was proud of Jory, that his CD had been nominated, but he wished it hadn't happened now.

"Did you hear the news?" Jory asked Harry.

"I did," Harry said. "You'd have to be living on another planet, not to. Congratulations."

"Thanks, ah, it means that I will have to relocate, transfer to another treatment center." Jory waited for a reaction.

Harry was looking at Dax. "And you're not happy about that?"

"Huh? Me. I've got no say in this. I didn't say anything," Dax muttered.

"You didn't have to. It's written all over your face. Are you going with him?" Harry asked.

What the fuck? He wasn't in therapy. "No," he said. "I'm not."

Harry looked at Jory. "We were talking about the reason you drank last time. You weren't happy when you left here. You seem better today."

"Dax and I discussed some things," Jory said.

We did a lot more than discuss.

"I think I understand myself better," Jory said.

What a bunch of horseshit. Jory was really putting on an act.

"So, I'm still not sure of the source," Harry said. "You seem anxious to get back to LA. Is it the limelight you miss or Ben?"

"Ben and I will be living apart."

Dax blinked. *Okay, that was new.*

"He will go on being my manager. We are taking a break." Jory looked at his hands.

Harry drank some water. "Any chance of a reconciliation?"

"Ben wants to go to couple counseling. We'll see, that's all." Jory yawned. "Sorry, I didn't get much sleep last night. Listen, can you find me a good counselor in LA. I don't want to miss any sessions."

"Sometimes that's hard to manage with a hectic schedule," Harry said. "Can you not put off going to LA for a couple more months?"

"I'm sorry," Jory said. "Can't."

Again, Harry looked at Dax. "You're quiet. Anything to contribute?"

"Jory is an adult. He makes up his own mind." Dax met Harry's gaze. "Do you really need me to be here? I'd like some air."

"Jory?" Harry said.

"Go, no problem," Jory said.

"I'll ah . . . come back to pick you up at three," Dax said.

"I'll find my own way," Jory told him.

Dax walked out of the office. He got into the car and pulled out his phone. It was supper time in Vancouver. Freda answered after two rings. "There you are. Hello, baby, you okay?"

"I will be. Listen, there's been a change of plans. I'm coming home."

"I thought Jory had two more months?"

"He's transferring his treatment to LA." He tried to keep the emotion out of his voice.

"Why? That's not a good idea, is it?"

"He's an adult. His CD has been nominated for an award,

and he needs to get back. He'll be fine." Something hard settled in his throat.

"I hear that heartbreak," she said softly.

He couldn't speak. He didn't for a moment.

"Dax?"

"Yeah. I'm here. I'll let you know what flight. Meet me at
the airport?"

"Of course. Love you. Honey, have you called Castor?"

"We've been texting back and forth. I'll see him when I
come home. I was going to go to a meeting here, but I didn't.
I'd rather see Castor."

"He's been asking me about you, been in the club a few
times. Are you feeling okay?"

"Still sober," he told her. "I need to get back. We'll talk
when I get there. Miss you."

"Me, too. Miss you. Kisses. Bye."

He sent Castor another text.

Hey.

Hey, Dax, my man. How are you?"

Not so good.

Take a breath. Find the source.

I know the source.

Jory?

He's going to LA early. Award. He's going to transfer.

Can he handle it?

I don't know.

Can you handle it?

No. I'm terrified.

You love him. Did you tell him?

Many times. Sometimes love isn't enough. I know the power of
fame.

And there's no way he can have that fame and you, too. He still
needs to choose. And you don't want him to make that choice.

It's not fair. If he chooses me, I'll always feel as if I held him back.
He may end up hating me for it. If he chooses fame, well . . . looks

like he has already.

So, come back to Vancouver, Dax, give him the divorce and make the break. This is killing you inside. It will hurt for a while but stop dragging it out.

This could set him back.

Don't say anything yet. Let him go. Come home, wait a little while, then send the papers. Your marriage has hit a dead end. You have done everything you could. Now, it's up to him. You are not responsible if he starts drinking again. You hear me?"

"Yes. Thanks, Castor. Talk later.

He turned off his phone.

The house was empty when he got there. He sat downstairs and fell asleep. When Jory came home, he was checking for flights to Vancouver.

Jory walked in, raised a hand. "Hey."

"Hey."

"Ah, everything is set. I will be at a new clinic in Beverly Hills next Monday, and the condo Ben rented for me is just down the street."

"Everything is falling into place," Dax said. "Good luck." He looked back at his phone.

"What are you doing?" Jory asked him, leaning against the wall.

"I'm trying to decide what flight to take back to Vancouver."

"Oh." Jory shrugged. "Maybe I'll come visit you sometime, in Vancouver."

Dax raised an eyebrow. He didn't comment.

"So, you're going to have to be with me a lot until you leave because I have no treatments until I get to LA. I might need you, like" —he cleared his throat—"in the middle of the night."

Dax's head went up. "I can't believe you." He got to his feet.

Jory looked at his feet. "I mean I . . ." He looked at him.

"Just that, it's not easy to leave you. I feel like we reconnected."

"Don't ask me to be your friend, Jory. My commitment to you is now done, so just go and get your award, live your life, be with Ben or whoever you want, but stay sober, and healthy, okay?" He placed a hand on Jory's shoulder.

Jory covered it with his. "And you stay healthy." He met his gaze.

Dax moved on. Jory's hand slid off his shoulder.

"I intend to do that," Dax said softly.

The best thing was to keep his distance from Jory. Jory was busy texting and talking to people on the phone about the upcoming award show. While he was occupied, Dax managed to book an earlier flight.

The next day came and it was time for Dax to let Jory and Susan know that he was leaving that afternoon. Freda would meet him tonight at the airport. He'd get in after midnight.

That morning, he drank his coffee slowly while Jory texted on his phone.

"Jory, can you stop that for a moment?" Dax asked him.

"Sure, sorry." He turned off his phone. "A lot to do."

Dax nodded. "Listen"—he looked at Susan—"I managed to get a flight out this afternoon."

Susan's jaw dropped.

Jory met his gaze. "So soon?"

He shrugged. "You don't need me here. Freda is overwhelmed. A lot of tourists."

He didn't intend to explain more than that.

"I'll take you to the airport," Jory offered.

"No need. I have the rental. I'll turn it in there." Dax got up. He looked at Susan. Tears ran down her face. He hugged her. "I'll miss you, too," he said softly, then left the kitchen.

His bag was packed. He checked the time. He'd leave a little early. As he was coming out of the room that had been his bedroom for the last three months, he came face to face with Jory.

"You leaving now? You have time," Jory said.

"No." He checked his watch unnecessarily. "There's no more time, Jory. I've tried to make up for everything. I think I have. We're even, right?"

Jory swallowed. "Yeah, more than even. Thank you. You probably saved my life."

"Okay, can we, can you move?" Dax asked. Jory was blocking the doorway.

"I'm trying. My feet feel like lead. Dax?" Jory searched his face.

Dax stroked his hair. He smiled at him. "It's all right, Jory. It's all right." He leaned down and kissed him softly on the mouth. Gently, he moved Jory aside and walked past. He hated these long goodbyes.

Jory didn't come upstairs. Susan hugged him tight at the door. "Jory," she began, but Dax shook his head.

"No more," he said. "It's okay." He kissed her cheek. "Look after him."

In the car, Dax took one last look at the house, he turned on the engine and pulled out of the driveway. On the way to the airport, he switched on the radio. There was the song.

Time stands still when I'm not in your arms. You stand on the precipice of my heart. Hold me like before, and it will be all right. I'll never leave your side. Baby, I need you tonight.

He'd only caught the end of it.

"Jory Carter," the DJ said, "with the hit song, *Never Leave You,* from his Grammy-nominated CD."

Dax turned off the radio.

On the plane, his head started pounding. He closed his eyes at one time and drifted off into one of those half sleeps.

He saw Jory's face. It was something he remembered from right after they were married. They'd been apart a few weeks. Jory met up with him at a concert in some city he couldn't recall. He came backstage and dragged Dax into a broom closet. Jory pulled off his clothes in the dark, kissing him everywhere and taking them both down to the floor. *God, Dax, I've missed you so much.* They'd barred the door with something. There were people outside trying to get in, but they paid no attention. The feel of Jory's mouth and hands, being inside of him, all of that caused his eyes to snap open. For a second, he thought they were still there in that closet.

He reached out his hand. But Jory wasn't beside him. He was alone, and he was getting so damned tired of being alone, dreaming of a man that wanted something else.

"You created a monster," Freda had told him once. "When you gave Jory a taste for fame, you lost him."

She was right. Dax never thought helping Jory's career would mean the end of them.

When he got off the plane, he was tired in every way, physically and emotionally. When he saw Freda running towards him, dressed in a flowery cotton dress and high heels, hoop earrings dangling down from her upswept hair, he smiled for the first time since he'd left New York.

He lifted her off her feet, twirling her around. People smiled, thinking they were a couple. She kissed him several times, then frantically wiped at his face to get the lipstick off. She linked arms with him. "I've missed you so much. You look great. Sad?"

He shook his head. "Not anymore. Let's go to the club. I want to see everyone."

"Your wish is my command, my prince," she said, laughing. "Luggage?"

"Just this bag," he said. "I travel light?"

When they turned the corner, they were hit directly in the

face by flashbulbs.

"Dax, Dax, is it true that you and Jory Carter are back together? Are you going to the Grammy's when your husband is — what do you think about Intoxication breaking up?"

Intoxication was breaking up? Damn.

There were too many cameras and microphones. Dax put up a hand. "One at a time, please."

One reporter put the mic in front of his face. "Hey, Dax, you look wonderful."

He nodded. "Thanks."

"How do you feel about Jory's nomination?"

"I'm happy for him, next?"

"Are you back together?" someone else asked.

"No."

"You were seen together in several places in New York City. Is it true he was there for Rehab?"

"No comment," Dax said.

"Any truth to the rumors that you will take part in a reunion concert with Intoxication?"

"I haven't been asked," he replied. "Now, if you'll excuse me." He pushed through the throng, whisking Freda to the parking lot. Some reporters ran after them, taking pictures.

When they were in the car, Dax sat back in the passenger seat and closed his eyes. "Like a pack of wolves. Damn."

Freda carefully pulled out of the parking space. "Now that Jory is nominated, I guess they wanted to track you down." She glanced at him. "They are relentless."

"We were spotted together in New York," Dax said, rubbing his eyes. "I suppose some people recognized us and took pictures, tried to sell them to the tabloids."

"How are you, honey?" She put a bejeweled hand over his.

"Exhausted."

"I'm glad you're back." She squeezed his hand.

"Me, too."

"If you want to talk about it, I'm here, darling," she said, turning off onto the road.

He smiled at her. "I know. Maybe tomorrow."

He fell asleep in the car. When he opened his eyes, Freda was looking down at him. "Hey, where am I?" He sat up. He saw all the frilly pink stuff and laughed. Freda lived in an apartment over the Club. "Oh. How did you get me up the stairs?"

"Muscles," she said, grinning. "Tried to put you in my bed, preferably naked, but didn't want to press my luck. You've been sleeping for almost twenty hours."

"Oh boy, feels like it, too." His back was killing him. "What time is it?"

"Around four in the afternoon." She plunked herself onto the sofa and lit a cigarette.

"Almost time to open the Club." He sat up, put his feet on the floor, and waved his hand in front of his face. "What is that you're smoking now? Looks like a cigar. Thought you were giving those things up. They'll kill you."

"With all the other chemical shit I put into my body every day, darling, to keep my feminine charm, this is the least of my worries. Hungry?"

"Coffee first. I'd take you to dinner, but we don't have time. I'd like to be there to open up tonight."

"Aw, I would have put on something sexy." She winked.

He laughed, looking at her pink, puffy slippers and silky bathrobe. "We could do pizza."

"Okay, but later, and you're paying since you put a real damper on my love life these last two nights." She pretended to make an angry face. She had never been very good at that when it was directed at him.

He winced. "Oops."

"It was more than oops, lover. I brought a real cutie up here last night. He asked me who you were, got one look at you and we ended up watching old videos of Intoxication half the night."

Dax sighed. "He recognized me. Sorry."

"Yeah, you look it," she scoffed. "But you did me a favor. He turned out to have a very tiny cock."

"Oh," Dax nodded, holding back a smile. "We can't have that."

"Well, we can but it's not memorable. In fact, I've forgotten his name." She stood up.

"Because of his tiny cock?"

"Darling" — she waved at him — "I am not that shallow."

Dax stood, trying not to laugh. "No, not you."

"And there you were, as a comparison, I couldn't help but be let down," she told him, coming over and kissing his cheek.

"Aw," he said, grinning. "Thank you."

She put her hands on his shoulders, met his gaze. "That Jory doesn't realize what he's giving up. You have it all, darling. He will regret his decision."

Dax sucked in some air. "I can't blame Jory for being excited about the award."

"You'd forgive that man anything, including the fact that he hopped into bed with Attila, the manager."

"That's over."

"Really?" She looked at him. "He has a new manager, too, then."

"I . . . don't know. I don't think so. I mean, they aren't going to live together anymore, for now." Even Dax was convincing himself as he spoke.

"I see," she mused. "Anyway, I'm sure he was excited about the award but Dax, if he'd wanted to, someone else could have accepted the award for him if he won."

"I know, but —"

"I've seen awards picked up by someone else," she said. "How many times did you not show up, Dax, to get an award?"

"That was different. At one point, they didn't mean anything and sometimes I was too wasted to bother attending. But this is his first time."

Freda stroked his cheek. "You've done all you could for that husband of yours. Maybe it's time you both move on." She patted his cheek. "You need to shave, baby."

"I know," he replied. "I should go home, take a shower, shave, and change my clothes."

"At least tell me you reconnected." She folded her arms across her chest.

"You know I don't kiss and tell," he said, walking by her. "Call me a taxi. I'll meet you at the Club in an hour."

"An hour, better make it two, it takes me that long to put my makeup on."

"Love you," he said. "I'll wait downstairs."

Dax could have walked to his apartment from where Freda lived, but it was raining, and he was still a little jet lagged. The FreDax, named for Freda, whose name was once Fred, with the addition of his name was on Granville Street, two blocks north of where he lived, and now enormously popular.

The addition of the live bands in the last two years had attracted more and more people, and just before he left for New York, the media was coming around to interview them, realizing who Freda's partner was.

Tonight, after he walked in, the staff all came to greet him with hugs and kisses. They were like a family, and they'd really missed him. Maybe they thought he wasn't coming back. Katy was the rock, a middle-aged woman with a will of steel, very experienced in management. She had opened tonight to let in the staff. They still had an hour or so before patrons would be admitted.

"Freda hasn't arrived yet. You know the madame," Katy joked.

Dax smiled. "Yeah, I know. I'm starved. I want pizza."

"Do you want me to order some?" Katy asked.

"No, I'll wait."

"If you want to check the books, I left everything for you in the back. I invited Lacy and the Frills back for the weekend."

"Good, I'd like to book them for longer," Dax said. "They're popular."

"I'll see what I can do," Katy said, telling one of the bartenders to make sure there were enough lemons. "Get some in the back," she said. "They've arrived."

Dax walked up to the bar and Bryan, one of the waiters, pushed an icy glass of Club Soda towards him. "How was New York?"

"Cold," he said, picking up the glass and taking a sip.

"We missed you," Bryan said.

Dax smiled. "Thanks. How are your courses going at the University?"

He nodded. "Good. I was going to ask you or Freda about extra shifts come summer?"

"We are always busy, so I don't see why not. Let me know when you need the extra hours, okay?"

"You're the best, Dax."

"Don't flatter him too much," a voice boomed, "I have to work with him."

There was some laughter.

Dax turned to look at Freda, all made up, walking in shoes with heels so high, it made him cringe. She was wearing a snug, sequined dress in a beautiful shade of blue. "Save me a dance later?" Dax grinned.

"Never mind that." She waved at him. "Bryan, you know Dax is like putty with you people. That's why nothing happens without my approval?"

Bryan saluted. "Yes, madame."

Dax folded his arms across his chest. "Can he have extra

hours?"

"Of course," she said, reaching over and pinching Bryan's cheek. "Too cute, that's why I hired him." She turned Dax around. "Look at him. These leather pants are enough to give someone a heart attack. Why don't you take him home, honey?"

"Freda." Dax shook his head.

"I tried." Bryan smiled at Dax. "He likes to play hard to get, something about me working here."

"Poo, poo," she said, looking at Dax. "Where's the pizza?"

"Katy said she'd order when you arrived," Dax said. "My stomach is growling."

Freda walked off to the office.

Dax gave Bryan back the glass. When he did, Bryan put his hand over his. Their eyes met. "Any time," Bryan said softly.

Dax smiled. "Thanks."

By the time he and Freda ate pizza in the back room, and Dax chastised her about encouraging Bryan, the patrons had started coming in. The DJ was playing some of today's popular dance hits and the evening had begun.

As he sat finishing his supper, Katy poked her head in. "Dax, someone here to see you. Says her name is . . . wait for it . . . Cookie Monster."

Dax's eyes widened. "Holy shit, really?"

"Who is she?" Freda asked, reapplying her bright red lipstick in the mirror.

"Luke's daughter." Dax got to his feet.

"Luke, as in Luke Wheeler, lead singer for Intoxication?" Katy practically squealed.

"That would be the one," he said. "Where is she?"

"I can bring her here," Katy said.

"Okay."

Freda looked at him. "I'll go out there." She narrowed her eyes. "What do you think she wants?"

He shrugged. "Don't know."

When Katy brought Elly Wheeler, AKA, the Cookie Monster, to the door, Dax took a step back. He'd been seventeen when he joined the band, and she'd been ten years old. Now she was nineteen.

"Dax!" Elly called out, running over and embracing him. "My God, you look the same, only better."

"Elly, wow, you've grown up. You're gorgeous," he said, smiling. She was tall and slim with long blonde hair. She had Luke's blue eyes. "What are you doing here?"

"I found out you co-owned this place. I wanted to see you." She took his hands. "Now, I remember why I had such a crush." She grinned. "You're so gorgeous, and you look well, Dax."

"Thanks. How's your dad?"

Her smiled faded. "Not good."

"Is he sick?" He led her over to the sofa. She sat down beside him.

"Too many parties," she said, "too many women, and the booze, the drugs. His heart isn't good. Liver is failing, too."

"Sorry to hear that." He truly was. Luke was a great talent.

"He wants you to be a part of the reunion tour, Dax." Elly met his gaze. "He won't ask you himself. He's too proud. But he's changed a lot from when you were with the band. He's over forty now, slowing down. He tells everyone that you leaving the band was the worst thing that had ever happened. He regrets it, Dax. Intoxication went downhill without you."

"It wasn't all his fault," Dax admitted. "He was older, had his own ideas about things, and maybe needed the fame more than I did. Egos got in the way. I was young, rebellious, and wild when I signed on as lead guitarist. Wasn't easy to have a young guy up front with him."

She smiled. "I remember being on tour with the band in the summer. You were so much fun, always had time to spend with me. You and Jory."

Dax squeezed her hand. He nodded, remembering. Elly had been just left with Luke. Her mother, a rich girl, who'd sowed her oats as a groupie to the band, married someone her family approved of and just disappeared. After that, Luke had a series of women, all who tried to be a mother to Elly because they wanted Luke to marry them. He never did.

"I'm so sorry it didn't work out with you two," Elly said. "I remember how much in love you were."

"Things change. How about Reggie? Does your dad stay in touch with him?"

"Reggie is the drummer for a lot of different bands now, has done some studio work. Jack plays bass with him sometimes. He harvests pot now in this country," she said.

"Sounds like an ideal job for Jack." He'd never seen the guy when he wasn't stoned.

"They all want in on the tour. I know it will be Dad's last, Dax." She came closer. "Please. I want it to be a success. It will be if you're with them."

"I can't just make the decision now, honey." He sighed, feeling under pressure. "There are a lot of good guitarists out there who—"

"Dad wants you. He wants the band back together, the way it was in the glory years." She dug a card out of her purse. "My number. Call me. I'll be in Vancouver for a few days. Maybe we can have lunch?" She paused. "I'm still your little Cookie Monster."

He laughed. "Are you still eating those cookies they made in London?"

"Yes," she said. "You can get them in LA now."

"Good."

"Just how much was it to ship those cookies?" she asked.

"You don't want to know."

She squeezed his hand. "I never forgot that. Someone is

waiting for me at a table. Come and say hello later?"

"Will do." He stood, hugging her. She kissed him on the cheek. "Love you, Dax."

He smiled. "Love you, too, kid."

Dax watched her walk out and slumped back down on the sofa. He closed his eyes a minute. He could see Jory chasing Elly around backstage before a concert. They'd play hide and seek. She loved that. She'd earned the name, Cookie Monster, from Dax, after Luke had bought these cookies in London. They were smothered in dark chocolate. Luke called them his fuel. They were really what he ate when he was high and had the munchies. One night, Elly got into the cookies and ate all of them. Luke was pissed. They were in Munich. Dax sent one of the crew members out to find the cookies. No, they were only available in London, so Dax bulk ordered the cookies. It cost him a fortune to have them flown to their hotel suite. When the cookies arrived, Luke and Elly made friends again. Dax gave Elly a box of cookies and dubbed her The Cookie Monster. It stuck.

When he heard Freda's voice, Dax opened his eyes.

"There you are," she said. "Everything all right?" She came and sat opposite him.

"Luke Wheeler's health is failing," he said.

"I'm not surprised. Saw him on the music awards. Both he and Reggie Brock looked like death. Jack Shepard wasn't there."

"Luke wants me to go on tour with them this last time. Elly said he was too proud to ask."

"Did he send her?" Freda asked.

"I think so."

"How do you feel about that?"

"Not sure. I have no idea how long the tour is. The last thing I want is to be back on the road. I really think they could find a good replacement. They've had two other lead guitar-ists."

"Dax." She leaned forward. "I don't want you to go away, but honestly, the fans will want it to be you. That will make the tour, sell the tickets."

Dax didn't comment. He knew that Intoxication was at the top when he was with them. It slipped when he left, but there were other reasons, too. He felt obligated to Luke. He took him on, chose him out of many others who'd auditioned. Yet he was leaning toward turning it down. "It's not because I don't think I can handle it," he told Freda, "that I'll be tempted to fall off the wagon. It's just that I really don't want to get on that hamster wheel again."

"And yet?" Freda persisted.

"I miss performing."

"That's why," she said, "we should only have live bands here, and you could head your own, do your own thing."

"With who? And then if I start a band, we'll be hounded by record companies, and producer and—no way."

"Just say no," she said. "Just perform here, and if you want to do a concert, do it on your own terms."

"Doesn't work like that, sweetie. It's a business, too many people involved." He stood. "I'll go out and see Elly, meet her friends."

"One of them is her boyfriend, seems like. They're kissing out there. I think you know him." Freda met his eyes.

Dax quirked an eyebrow. "Who?"

"Reggie Brock."

Dax blinked. "The Reggie Brock?"

"If it's not him, it's his double."

"He's twice her age."

"Love is blind. He is kind of cute, in a rock star ravished way."

Dax headed to the door. "Jesus." He opened the door and

was hit by a blast of electronic dance music. He made his way through the crowd of dancers and looked around. When he saw Elly and Reggie, he took a breath. Wow. Life was strange. Oh well, who was he to judge?

Reggie got to his feet when he saw Dax. "Hey, buddy," he called out, swaying a bit. There were several empty glasses of something on the table.

Reggie was drawn in the face, his dyed blond hair hanging past his shoulders. A ring in his nose and one in the left eyebrow. He was wearing purple leggings and a knee-length black jacket. It was halfway open, revealing several silver chains hanging off his neck and a tattoo of two drum sticks on each side of his collar bone.

Dax embraced him. "Hello, Reggie," he said. "How are you doing?"

He shrugged. "Slowing down. Shit," he said, slapping Dax on the arm. "You look fucking great, but then you're what now, twenty-four, five?"

"Twenty-six next month."

"Just a baby," he said, sitting down. He took Elly's hand. "I'm very lucky to have my lady here. She keeps me honest." He lifted a hand to the waiter as Dax sat down. "A double scotch for me, wine for my lady, and anything Dax wants. I'm going to buy you a drink," he said.

The waiter hesitated.

"It's okay, Marty," Dax told him. "Bring me some ice water."

The waiter walked away.

Reggie eyed him. "I'm trying to be friends here, man."

"Reggie, I don't drink. I'm an alcoholic." Dax looked at him.

Reggie grinned. "Hell, so am I, man. If you're an alcoholic, you might as well earn the reputation."

Elly didn't say a word. She just looked around like she

wanted to escape.

"I'd rather go on living," Dax said. "I never did care much about my reputation."

Reggie laughed. "That's true. Dax here was the wild one. Then he went and married that singer, Jory, what was his last name?" He looked at Dax.

"Carter," Dax said.

"Let a guy blow me once," Reggie said. "Really good at it but I prefer a gentler mouth." He smiled and leaned over to kiss Elly.

"Stop, Reg," Elly told him.

The waiter brought the drinks.

Dax glanced at her, but he didn't say anything.

"So, guess Elly told you about the reunion. What do you think, kid?"

Kid? They'd called him that when he joined the band. "I don't think so," he said. Since he'd seen the shape Reggie was in, he was even more convinced.

Elly did speak then. "Dax, you promised to think about it."

"I did," he said. "You can find another guitarist."

"Listen," Reggie said, draining his glass, then pointing at him. "There is no one better out there than you. You are the best, my man. We always knew that. Luke screwed it up because when you came on board, suddenly, the chicks were ripping off their tops for you, not Luke. It bruised his ego. But when you walked, we knew it was the death knell. The chicks were coming to see you, man. And so were the boyfriends. When you played that guitar, it was magic. The girls, they wanted in your pants and the guys, well, they just wanted to be you, Dax. We need you. The tour won't fly without you. Talk to Luke."

Dax took a sip of his water. "That's ancient history. I don't care about that."

"Listen, the shows will only be in select cities in the US,"

Reggie said. "No more than six or eight months if the arenas sell out." He put a hand on Dax's forearm. "Come on, man. We need you." He stood, motioned to Elly. "Come, baby, let's dance."

"Not right now," she said. "I'd like to talk to Dax."

He reached out and grabbed her arm. "Now," he grunted.

Dax sprang up from his seat. He pulled Reggie back as Elly rubbed her arm. "Don't you ever do that again. She said no."

Reggie pulled away. Dax remembered what an ugly drunk he was. "She's my girlfriend, man. She'll do what I say."

Dax stood there, maintaining eye contact. "And this is my club. Get out."

Reggie reached for Elly again. Dax grabbed his arm, pulled it around back, and lead him to the door. He was struggling, but he was too drunk. Dax handed him over to the doorman. "See that he leaves."

"Elly?" he cried out as the doorman pushed him outside.

Elly came running toward Dax. "Where is Reggie? I have to find him because he'll be angry."

Dax put his hands on her shoulders. "What's going on? What are you doing with him anyway? Are you afraid of him?"

"When he's sober, he's good," she said, wiping her tears. "He's sick, Dax. He's almost as sick as Dad. Have pity."

"He did this to himself. You don't have to pay for that. You can stay with me for a while. Let him go, okay?" He waited for her to answer.

Slowly, she nodded. "Okay. My stuff is at the hotel, though."

"I'll take you. Just let me tell Freda, okay?"

Thankfully, Reggie was not at the hotel when Dax took Elly there to get her things. He brought her back to his place and led her into the guest room. "You can have this room tonight, Elly."

"Thanks, Dax. Are you going back to the club?"

"I'll stay if you want," he said.

"No, it's okay. I'm tired. I'm going to bed."

"Are you all right?" he asked her.

She hugged him. "Thanks."

Elly stayed with him a few days. She spoke with Reggie a few times on the phone, finally convincing him that it was over. Dax drove her to the airport. She took a flight back to LA. Two days later, Dax got a phone call from Elly. "Dax, my dad wants to talk to you."

"Okay," he said. "Put him on."

"Dax? It's Luke."

"Hello, Luke. How are you doing?"

"Okay, not bad. Listen, I wanted to thank you for making Elly see sense. Reggie and Elly weren't a good mix. I was against it from the start."

"Elly made up her own mind."

"Yeah, but you looked after my little girl. You did that when she was a kid, too. I wasn't the greatest Dad."

"You did your best."

"You know I need you."

Dax sighed.

"Please, think about it. This is my final hurrah. I want to do this with you. I want the fans to remember this. They want you. So do I. Please Dax, there is still a month before we need your final commitment. Think about it."

"I have. I'm sorry. I wish you the best, Luke," he said and hung up.

He woke up dreaming about Jory most every morning. He kept hoping Jory would call or send him an email. He hadn't heard a word from him in almost three months. He would have liked to know how his treatment went. All he knew was that Jory was working on a new CD in LA.

Freda stopped by that morning with coffee and bagels. He was still half asleep. "Too early?" she asked, kissing him.

"I didn't sleep well last night." He took the coffee. "Thanks."

"You look tired. What's bothering you? I thought you'd already made your decision about going out on tour?" She opened the lid of her coffee and blew on it.

"I spoke to Luke, told him no."

"Are you having second thoughts?" Freda put the bag of bagels on the counter.

"No. I've made up my mind about that."

"But you feel guilty because you are a softie." Freda kissed him on the cheek.

Dax fell quiet and drank his coffee.

"And you miss Jory?" She opened the bag and took out the bagels.

He looked at her. "It shows?"

"Of course. Why don't you call him?"

"He hasn't called me." He took the bagel.

"He's working in studio now." Freda bit into the bagel. "Is he back with Ben?"

"You tell me. You seem to know." Dax looked at her.

"I read a lot of magazines." She shrugged.

"I don't want to know."

"Okay. What about his mother? Have you heard from her?"

"No."

"You could call and ask her how Jory is." Freda waited for him to reply.

He shook his head. "Not going to happen."

"Okay, let's change the subject. So." She pointed to a pile of mail on the counter. "You don't read your mail anymore?"

"It's always a lot of ads," he said. "Royalty statements. My bills are all paperless now."

"I like that." Freda walked over to the pile of papers. "Travel magazine." She picked it up. "Can I read it?"

"Sure."

Some of the mail fell on the floor. She picked it up. "Ah, Dax, there's something here that looks important. Maybe you should open this." She handed him a manila envelope. "It's a law firm in LA."

Dax narrowed his eyes. He put down the bagel, wiped his hands, and got to his feet. "What?"

"Says" — Freda read the envelope out loud — "Danick and Seburg, Attorneys at Law."

Dax took the envelope from her. He stared at it, looked at Freda.

"Do you want me to give you some privacy?" she asked, pursing her lips.

"No," he said, ripping it open. The heading said Petition for Divorce. He stared at it for a long time, flipped it to the last page, and read the signature. *Jory Carter.* He went over and sat it on the counter. There was a typewritten note. *Dear Dax. Let's end this charade. I don't love you anymore. So, sign the papers. Jory.*

Dax crumpled the note in his fist and threw it on the floor.

Freda walked over and looked at the document. "Dax? Oh, Dax, I'm so sorry."

Dax put up his hand. He couldn't speak. It was over, finally over, between them. That was why Jory hadn't called him. He wanted to be free. He'd lied to him, told him he loved him, for what? For a fuck?

He wasn't going to shed tears. He looked at Freda. "I've been an idiot. Even after Jory went back to LA, I thought maybe there was a chance for us, especially after . . ." He trailed off.

"After what?" Freda asked him. There were tears in her eyes.

"He broke up with Ben and we . . ." He cleared his throat.

"All he wanted from me was a fuck. That was it. Maybe that was all our marriage was about."

"Oh, no, honey, I can't believe that."

"I'm not going to let this kill me," he said. "It's for the best." He picked up his cell phone and dialed.

Freda watched him, coming closer, a curious expression on her face. "Who are you—"

A voice answered, "Dax? Hey, what's up?"

"I've changed my mind," Dax said. "I'm going on tour."

Freda's eyes widened.

"That's great, man," Luke said. "I'll be in touch soon to let you know the arrangements."

"Okay," Dax told him and hung up. He tossed the phone aside.

"Are you sure, Dax?" Freda asked. "In your state right now, maybe touring isn't the best idea."

His first instinct was to get angry, tell her to stop mothering him, but instead, he opened his arms and hugged her. "I need this right now. If I stay here, there's not enough of a distraction. I'll go crazy. I promise I won't stray." He put her out of his reach and smiled. "I'll stay sober. No one or nothing is worth killing myself for. This is the last of Intoxication. We're going to go out in a blaze of glory. I'm going to make sure of it."

Freda reached up and wiped a single tear off Dax's cheek. "You'll stop loving him, Dax, one day."

He walked over to the counter, took off his wedding band, and set it on the counter. He looked at Freda. "This is the first step. I need some air. When I get back, I'll sign the papers."

CHAPTER EIGHT

Jory looked up in surprise from where he sat in the middle of the living room floor. "Ben?" Jory said. "I thought you'd be working all day." He'd come here in the middle of the day to go through some of his stuff thinking Ben wouldn't be home.

"Came back early. I'm happy to see you," Ben said. "Are you back to stay?"

"No, I was just going through some things I'd put into boxes a month or so ago. I'd like to take them home now."

Ben nodded. He sat down. "So, you going to buy that house?"

"That, or another one."

"I've made a mess of things, haven't I?"

"We both have," Jory said. And he wasn't just talking about Ben. He'd left New York in early March, and it was almost July. He'd heard nothing from Dax. Not a word. Dax hadn't contacted his mother either. God, he missed him so much. He poured himself into his work, writing song after song, none of which seemed to be good enough to go on the CD. At night he lay awake thinking of the last time they'd been together, how Dax had made love to him, how his cock felt, his skin, how he tasted. Damn, he'd messed up everything. He should have never let him go.

"Jory?" Ben touched his shoulder.

Jory looked up at him. "Yeah."

"We could see a counselor."

"What for, Ben?" Jory sighed, got up off the floor. "We are over. We probably should have never gotten together."

"Jory? Please, listen, baby, I—"

Jory put up his hand. "Ben, I love Dax. I always have and always will. Even if he doesn't want to be with me anymore. You drove him away. Actually, you used him and threw him away because you wanted to be with me. I was vulnerable, out of my mind, and you were convenient. I never loved you. You know that."

"Yes, I know that," he snarled. "And I didn't care as long as you were in my bed and not his."

"You are obsessed with Dax, maybe because you could never have him himself. Was I the next best thing?'

Ben's anger flared. "Dax Franklin, seventeen and already on a path to self-destruction. No self-control. He's one of the best and yet he is too much of a weak-willed coward to be who he is because he is in love with the bottle. He made a pass at me once. He wanted me, but I knew what he was, an egotistical prick with a drinking problem. You didn't read the signs."

"You never knew him at all," Jory said. "And you made the pass. Dax told me all about it. You tried a few times until he told you to fuck off. He didn't want you. So, say what you want, believe what you will about Dax." He took a breath. Ben had turned his back.

"Where are my photographs? I had several photo albums, and I can't find them."

"If you're talking about all those pictures of you and that guitar player, I put them out with the trash."

Jory gasped. His heart fell to his feet. Those pictures were all he had left of Dax, along with the wedding band he kept in his jewelry box. All their wedding photos, pictures of Dax, some of them intimate and private. "You bastard," Jory breathed.

"I didn't think you wanted them anymore," Ben said.

Tears ran down Jory's face. "And where is my wedding

ring?"

He shrugged. "Didn't see it."

"You had no right," Jory hollered.

"It was a cheap piece of gold."

"You fucking son of a bitch. That ring meant the world to me."

"Oh, for Christ's sakes, I don't see Dax beating down your door, Jory. You and Dax are over. You have been for a long time. Get the fuck over it."

Jory walked right up to Ben and swung, hitting him hard in the mouth.

Ben backed up, touched his hand to his lip.

"I want my ring. You better find it. And I want a new manager. You're fucking fired. And don't you ever come near me again, Ben." Jory picked up the box. He pointed at him. "If you don't send someone with my wedding ring to my house before tomorrow morning, I'm charging you with theft." With that, he left.

The next day when Jory walked into the studio, someone came up and handed him a small box. "Came this morning by courier." Jory hurried into the bathroom and tore open the box. There was his ring. Tears filled his eyes. He hadn't worn it for a long time because it upset Ben. But Ben be damned now. He took it out and slipped it back on his finger.

He remembered when Dax had put it on. "With this ring, I thee wed." Jory looked into the mirror. He saw Dax's face, smiling. He smiled back. "Till death do us part," he whispered.

"Jory?"

The door opened, and one of the studio technicians walked in. "Someone said you'd be in here. What time do you want to start?"

Jory tossed the box into the garbage. "Ah, soon. Give me a

minute."

"Okay, you heard the news about your ex?" He paused before leaving.

"What news? Is Dax okay?"

He laughed. "Yeah, he's on tour with Intoxication. Going to be their last. The front man isn't doing so well."

Jory was speechless.

"You okay?"

"Just that I didn't think I'd ever see Dax back out there again. Ah, when did the tour start? What planet have I been on?"

"You've been here twelve hours a day, Jory. The tour started two weeks ago. They're doing the US. Someone told me it finishes next August, here in LA. The reviews are fantastic. Your ex is a wizard with the guitar."

Jory smiled. "I know that. I need to watch YouTube, catch a show. Maybe I can get to a concert. Can someone get me their tour schedule?"

"Sure."

"Okay, I'll be in the sound booth in a few minutes. Have someone tune my piano."

"Done," he said, leaving the bathroom. Jory leaned against the sink, folding his arms. On tour again? Dax? Jory wasn't sure how to make sense of that.

He sent his mother a text. *Hey, you there?*

Yes. Hello, honey, you okay?

Better than before.

What does that mean?

I fired Ben.

Good.

Mom, anything from Dax?

Why don't you call him?

He's on tour.

Vacation?

No. Touring with Intoxication.

No. Really???

Yes. Why hasn't he called? I thought he'd call me.

Maybe he was waiting for you to make some choices. He loves you.

I love him. I wish I could stop. I'll do anything he wants if he gives me a chance. I don't know what him being on tour means.

Find him. Ask him. Damn you guys deserve a second chance, Jory.

I know. Anyway, got to go. Kiss, kiss.

He put the phone back into his pocket. He was thinking about his mother's words. Second Chance. The words flowed right out of his heart. He grabbed a pen on the way down the hallway and walked into the studio. He held up his hand. "I need some time now. Come back in an hour." He was scribbling.

Second Chances. Wasted romances. In between, always you. I can't live without hoping for your second chances, touch me again, stay by my side. We will make love in the field, watch the birds fly, over you, over me. I can never let it be because, baby, baby, please, second chances is all I live for. Die for. Cry for. Second chances with you, only you can make my heart soar, touch the core of me, baby, please, let me die in your arms, let me spend the rest of my life looking into your eyes, give me, give me, second chances.

Jory was breathless. He swallowed hard, suddenly hearing the smattering of applause. "That was beautiful. Wait until your fans hear it."

Jory stood up. "There's only one person who needs to hear it." He sighed. "Someone needs to tell me where Intoxication is performing next and get me a plane ticket. I'm going to get my husband back."

There was more applause.

"Okay, get the rest of the musicians in here," Jory said, "so we can work on this song. I might be incognito for a while."

Intoxication was playing in Kansas tonight, but it was too late for Jory to get a ticket. Even with his connections, it was totally sold out. Two nights later, they'd be in Denver. He had his ticket to the show and for the plane. He practiced what he was going to say over and over. He was ready to make this work, no matter what he had to do.

Tonight, he curled up in bed and watched some clips from the concert they'd done in New Mexico. Dax looked and sounded great. The other guys were holding their own. They were playing to sold-out arenas, fans were singing along to some of the old favorites. Jory fell asleep with the television on.

When he woke up the next day, the television was back to the news channel. He sat up and looked at the screen. It looked like footage from an Intoxication concert. He turned up the volume. Then he read the caption. *Luke Wheeler, front man for Intoxication, collapses on stage, dead on arrival at the hospital.*

Oh no, Jory thought. He surfed the channels for more information. He found another. "This is breaking news. Intoxication Front man Luke Wheeler lost consciousness at a concert in New Mexico." In the corner, Jory could see Luke fall on his knees. Dax was right beside him. "We are waiting for confirmation as to the cause of death. People close to the rocker said he was expecting to undergo heart surgery after the tour. More on this story later."

Jory turned off the television. He needed to reach Dax. How horrible? Would the tour continue without Luke?

He heard his doorbell. His maid wasn't in today, so Jory hurried down the hall and answered the door. A courier stood there. He handed Jory an envelope and asked for a signature. When Jory opened the envelope, he stared at it. "Divorce papers?" He'd been looking for these. He'd left them with his stuff. He intended to rip them up. He didn't want a divorce. He was never going to send these. He couldn't remember if he'd signed them. Maybe he did when he was angry and drunk.

Ben must have sent them. He rifled through them, just to check if he signed them that time when he was in a mood. When he got to the last page, he almost dropped the papers. "What? No." At the bottom was his signature, and right beside it was Dax's.

He looked at the return address. These had been sent from Canada. They'd gone to the old address, then been redirected. Dax must have sent them just before he left on tour. Jory sunk down on the sofa. "Why, Dax?" he asked no one. "What does this mean?" He tossed them aside. They had to be filed in court, and it would take a long time. Ben told him ninety days. How in the hell had Dax gotten these papers? He hadn't sent them. Ben. They were signed so he sent them to Dax. He should have punched him harder.

He had to reach Dax. The question was, how? The band members were avoiding the press and surrounded by security. They'd canceled two concerts, but the media reported that the tour would continue as planned with the three original members. Dax was now front man for the band. Former lead guitarist Doug Lalonde was also to join the tour.

Anybody who was anyone in the music industry would be attending Luke Wheeler's funeral. It was a strange place to have a reunion, but Jory would have to wait to see Dax there.

Although there were many celebrities, the media was not invited. The service was held in Luke's mansion in Beverly Hills. His remains were to sit in a display case on a mantle looking out over the many awards Intoxicated had received over the years.

Jory arrived in a limo, with his new manager, Angela Reed.

The service was nice. Many people got up to speak, and there was a good portrait of Luke in the front. When Jory saw Dax walk up to the podium, a lump settled in his throat. It had been almost six months since he'd seen him in person. He looked wonderful, a little thinner. Jory closed his eyes when he heard his voice.

"Luke and I," he said, "we had our differences. Two generations of musicians, both stubborn, with their own ideas." There was laughter. "Luke loved music, and he loved his fans. We gained a new respect for each other on this tour. This life we live is often not long. On the stage, under the lights, we give everything to our fans and to our music. Luke did that. He wanted to go out with glory, and he did that, too. I will miss you, Luke. See you."

There was applause.

Jory saw a young woman run to meet Dax and hang on his arm. Who was that?

When Angela saw where he was looking, she said, "Luke's daughter, Elly."

"Oh my God, the Cookie Monster," Jory said.

Angela gave him a strange look.

"I'll tell you one day."

The reception was in the ballroom, just down the hall. Jory filed out with the rest, stopping to talk to some of the people he knew. This was his world, the rich and famous, hobnobbing with people he thought he'd never meet. And he owed that all to Dax. And really, all he wanted was to see him, speak with him.

It was at least an hour before Jory finally got close enough to Dax to get his attention. He was talking with some industry people Jory didn't know.

Dax noticed him. He stopped talking in mid-sentence. "Hello, Jory," he said. He sounded very formal, standing there in his dark blue suit.

"Nice speech."

"Thanks. I thought you'd show up." He came closer. "How are you?"

"Not so great."

"Oh?" He looked around. "Ben not here?"

"Why would he be?" Jory asked. "Angela Reed is my manager now."

"Good. I hear good things about her."

"Can we talk?"

"Jory?"

Reggie came over. "Is that you?"

"Hello, Reggie, yes, good to see you," Jory said.

Then Jack came over, too. Jory looked around, and Dax was gone. *Damn it.*

Finally, he met up with Elly, who hugged and kissed him. "So happy you're here, Jory. You look sensational. Does Dax know?"

"Yes, he's somewhere. Seen him?"

"He's probably outside. He doesn't like to be around all these people."

"I can't get over how big you are." Jory laughed.

"I can't get over you and Dax not being together." She looked sad. "Can't you fix it?"

"I'm trying, but it would help if I could find him."

"Come on, let's look for Dax," she said.

"Are you okay?" Jory asked as they walked down the hallway together. Jory stopped to admire the band photos, Dax in leather with his guitar.

"Yes. Dax saved me from a disaster. He and Dad made nice."

"Dax is a good one."

"Yeah. I was dating Reggie. I'm not good at picking boyfriends."

"I see. Anyone new?"

"If I didn't think you were the love of his life, or that he could be bisexual, it would be Dax. I've always been crazy about him. But he's yours."

"No, he's not. I mean." Jory sighed. "I'm really not sure anymore."

"Well, there he is on the balcony —" she pointed —"go find out." She gave him a push.

Jory walked out onto the balcony. "Hey," he said, closing the door.

Dax glanced at him. "Hey."

"You didn't call. You didn't text." Jory came to stand beside him. "You gave me a divorce."

"You sent the papers." He didn't look at him.

"No. I didn't."

Dax looked at him.

"Ben did. And he burned all our photos."

"I'll give you mine."

"You didn't burn yours?" Jory tried to laugh but couldn't.

"No."

Jory looked at his hand. "But you rook off your ring." He reached out and held up Dax's left hand.

"And you put yours back on." Dax shook his head. "What's going on, Jory? I got the papers and you'd signed them."

"That was a long time ago when I was angry, but I didn't send them. Ben must have —"

"I don't care anymore." Dax waved his hand.

"I love you."

"Stop it," Dax told him. "This is not the time or the place. Just, don't."

"But," Jory began, "Dax."

"Listen, I just watched a man die in front of me. I've got to finish this tour. He made me promise that if he couldn't go on, I would. I'm fighting the urge to drink all the time, and you're not helping things."

"The tour and the parties and —"

"No, it's not that. It's you. I want to drink because I'm trying to stop loving you. Just let me do that, okay, let me do it. We are a disaster, you and I. Go away, go talk to someone else. Fall in love with someone else." Dax brushed by him and walked inside.

When Elly came back out, Jory was holding back tears. "Didn't go well?"

"No."

"He's really upset. He tried to save my dad. And he's been letting me cry all over him for the past few days. Give him space. He's got a lot on his plate right now, leading this band and filling my father's shoes, but don't give up on him. I truly believe that you will be together."

"I'm leaving," Jory said. "Say goodbye for me. Tell him, no matter what he believes, I love him. I need him. I'll never stop. And if he needs me, I'm here." Jory scribbled down his address. "Tell him to come to me tonight so we can talk." *So, I can hold him again.*

She said she would, and Jory went home.

Jory paced the floor. At three in the morning, he tried to sleep. He couldn't. He looked out the window—nothing. Dax wasn't coming tonight or any night after.

Jory pulled on some clothes and left his house. He walked down the street two blocks and walked into the all-night liquor store. He bought a bottle of vodka. He wouldn't drink the whole thing, just a glass, something to help him sleep.

CHAPTER NINE

It was dawn and Dax was beat. It had been a hellishly long day. Elly told him to stay at the mansion instead of at the hotel. Dax figured she needed him to talk to. She took him to an upstairs bedroom. There was a balcony and they sat together watching the sun come up.

Elly had gone through an entire bottle of wine. They spoke about Luke and her childhood. "He was the one constant," she said. "A shitty dad but at least he was there. I have a brother, you know."

"No, I didn't. Luke never mentioned him."

"He told me a few months back, in case he, well, died." She swallowed.

Dax squeezed her hand. "He loved you, despite all his crap. And you should find your brother."

She nodded. "I will. Do you remember all those horrible girlfriends?" She shuddered. "He wanted me to call them mother."

"You used to number them, call them step-monster number one and two," Dax laughed.

"And seven," she laughed. "I missed you when you left." She met his gaze. "I loved you so much."

Dax didn't like the way this was headed. She was vulnerable and she was looking at him with longing in her eyes. She wasn't a little girl anymore.

"I had no choice," he said, thinking he should leave now.

She stood. "Dax?" She came over to his chair. "Would it be all right if —"

She tried to straddle his chair.

"No, Elly, no," he said, getting up and pushing her gently away. "This isn't going to happen. I'm sorry, honey. You are in a bad place. It wouldn't be right for me to take advantage of you."

She started to cry.

He held her for a few minutes. "So sorry, Elly."

"I know you love Jory and—" She stopped. "Oh damn, I forgot," she said, pulling a paper out of her pocket. "Jory gave this to me before he left. It's his address here in LA. He wanted you to go to him, talk."

Dax looked at the paper. "Doesn't matter anymore. It's over."

"You love him. Go. Don't mind me. Life is short, Dax. Work it out."

"I know we need to settle some things." He checked his watch. "I just couldn't handle it last night." He sighed. "Maybe I should try. It's a little early in the morning."

"I'm sure he's waiting for you," she said.

Elly gave Dax the address and told him to take one of Luke's cars. He wasn't sure what he was going to say to Jory, but it was time to make some decisions about their marriage or lack thereof. He was so confused and sad. His stress level was at an all-time high. They had to finish the tour. They had to do it in Luke's memory. He was feeling the pressure.

He found the address easily. When he got to the gate, he stepped out and looked around. He could barely see the house as it was concealed behind a high electronic fence. He pressed the buzzer. Nothing. He pressed it again, waited. There was no answer.

As he turned around, a car drove up. It was one of those private security companies. A man got out, short and stocky, in a beige uniform. "Good morning," he said. "Can I help you, sir?"

"I'm here to see Jory Carter, and he doesn't seem to be home. I was just about to leave." Dax headed back to Luke's Corvette. He didn't want to hang around. He'd heard some stories about over-enthusiastic security guards, and he was in no mood to get into any problematic situations.

"Hey" — the man stepped up to him — "you're Dax Franklin." His face broke out into a smile.

"Yes," Dax replied, reaching for the door. "That's me."

"I'm a fan," he said. "You are a great guitar player." He started playing air guitar and made some guitar-like sounds in his throat.

"Thanks." Dax tried not to laugh. Again, he reached for the door.

"So, you were right beside Luke Wheeler when he died, right? That must have been tough. Sympathies, man. I read you tried to save him, gave him mouth to mouth and stuff."

This was the last thing he wanted to revisit right now. "Yes, it was too late. I'm sorry, I have to go."

"Ah, hate to ask, but would you mind a picture with me and an autograph? My wife will be especially grateful if you know what I mean?" He winked.

"Sure," Dax told him, posing in front of the guard's cell phone. The man handed over his note pad. "You can sign right there," he said, grinning. "I'm not supposed to, you know, but you're Dax Franklin. I'd like to get Jory Carter's, too, but we don't seem to connect. He's gone most the time, guess he's not with that manager guy anymore. Shit, you two, still married, or what?"

Dax handed him back the notepad. "Why don't you ask Jory Carter? I have no fucking idea." This time he managed to get into the vehicle. He lifted his hand to the guard and drove off down the road.

Dax took the car back to Luke's home and parked it in the

garage. He ordered a rental car and one of the employees delivered it personally, for an extra fee. It was a five-hour drive to Las Vegas. He really didn't want to go with the band on the plane. He needed some space. He also was in desperate need of sleep.

When he went back inside Luke's house, everything was quiet. He returned to the room Elly had given him and lay down on the bed. He set his alarm so he wouldn't sleep too long. He thought he'd fall into a coma the minute his head touched the pillow but no chance.

He was on stage again, reliving everything. Luke seemed in fine form, lots of energy, and the audience was eating out of the palm of their hands. Then Luke just fell, one hand clutching his chest. He went to his knees. The music stopped.

Dax heard himself breathing hard, the adrenalin pumping. *Come on, Luke, come on. Come on.*

When the stretcher took Luke off stage, Dax knew that was the end. Everyone turned to him. What were they going to do now? They couldn't cancel the tour. The money, lawsuits, ticket sales, their careers, their everything. DAX.

His eyes opened. "Jory?"

He was alone. He sat up, running a hand through his hair. "Jory," he whispered. He just couldn't deal with seeing him earlier. He'd lost it. This game of I love you, I don't, I want a divorce, I don't. Let's talk, let's not talk for months. He couldn't take it anymore.

Now, he was sorry. He wanted to tell him that no matter what, he still loved him, but maybe he was just prolonging the pain. Finish it. They needed to do it for both their sakes.

Dax pulled that paper out of his pocket. There was a phone number. He dialed, waited. It rang five times. There was no voice mail so he couldn't leave a message. "Jory, where in the hell are you?" Maybe he should try again before he left for Las Vegas. He got out of bed, checked the time. It was three in the afternoon. He took a shower, changed his clothes. If there wasn't too much traffic, he could be in Las Vegas around ten o'clock, even with some breaks in between.

He sent a text to the road manager, telling him his plans. "See you there," he said. "I need some alone time."

Everyone was still sleeping. He'd text them all later.

The rental was an economy car, roomy, air-conditioned, with a good stereo system, nothing that would attract too much attention. Dax returned to the address in Beverly Hills that Elly had given him. He parked across from the electronic fence.

Dax went to the gate, rang the bell. Waited. No answer. "Damn it, Jory."

A middle-aged, blonde, woman came running up the road suddenly. She stopped, jogging in place. "Hi, my, my, but you're Dax Franklin."

"Yes."

"If you're looking for your husband, he left a few hours ago, went tearing out of here on two wheels in his Trans Am. I hear he's at the recording studio in Santa Monica most days now."

"Okay, thanks," Dax said, walking back to his car.

She smiled. "Didn't figure you for a family car, sweetie?"

"It's a rental," he told her, with a wink.

She laughed. "Bye, baby, have a good ride. Oh, you're even better looking in person if that's possible. See you in my dreams, honey."

"Have a good one," he told her and got into the car.

She ran off.

Dax went through the drive-through and got one of those breakfast sandwiches. They were now available twenty-four hours a day. A large coffee, and he was on the way to Las Vegas. He stopped in Bakersfield and sent a text to everyone who needed to know where he was. He didn't want anyone to panic. Everyone was on edge.

There was a room waiting for him at the Hard Rock Hotel when he arrived. He needed some sleep, along with food.

It felt good to be alone in the hotel suite before the guys arrived. He put the complimentary champagne in a drawer and settled in the hot tub. Room service was surf and turf, and he practically devoured his food.

Later in bed, he watched some mindless slasher film and answered a million text messages. He switched off the light, then thought about calling Jory again. He hunted for the paper and dialed the number. No answer. No voice mail either. In frustration, he threw the phone on the floor. "Forget it," he muttered, snuggled down into the pillow and fell asleep.

The following two days before the concert were hectic. On the morning of the performance, he'd been booked on an early morning talk show. He'd been told he had no choice but to be on the show. Fans needed to be reassured that the tour would continue without Luke Wheeler.

The road manager accompanied Dax to the studio in downtown Vegas in a limo. When he got out, there were tons of reporters, cameras going off in his face, and microphones shoved in front of him. He smiled and kept moving while security guards controlled the crowd. He hated this shit.

Inside, Dax breathed a sigh of relief, while Ivan Hoffman, his manager, fused over every detail. He was whisked to a back room where some coffee was pushed in his hand by a production assistant. Someone ran in and handed him a sheet with a bunch of questions. "Look them over and if there is anything you don't want to talk about, cross it out," she said.

Dax was trying to look over the questions, but people were running all over, telling him things he wouldn't remember. When things settled down, he ended up crossing out a bunch of things on the list, mostly to do with his relationship with Jory.

There was music playing now, the intro to the show, and the host, Brenda-Lee Asage, came out to do her opening monologue.

Dax watched on the monitor. She was well known, formally a hard-nosed reporter for Entertainment Beat Magazine. Now she had her own show, and it was popular.

"Today, we are very lucky to have Dax Franklin, front man for Intoxication, on the show."

There were some whistles and applause.

"Dax Franklin joined the band at the tender age of seventeen." A picture of him at that age appeared on a screen behind her, complete with leather pants, long hair, and open shirt.

Again, a reaction of appreciation from the audience.

"Yes, one can see why he was immediately considered the sex symbol of the band. Now, given the loss of Luke Wheeler, Dax is out front, where, some say, he should have been all along. We're going to talk to Dax about his life, career, and the loss of a rock icon, when we come back."

Applause.

A woman walked in the room with headphones. She motioned to Dax. "Ready, Mr. Franklin?"

He stood, nodded. "Let's do this," he said.

"Ladies and gentlemen," Brenda-Lee announced as Dax entered the stage, "please welcome, the one and only, Dax Franklin."

CHAPTER TEN

"God damn it, Juan, I told you to tape the Asage Morning show today."

"I did, Mr. Carter, sir." Juan came on a run into Jory's bedroom. "Would you like me to put it on for you now, sir?"

Jory threw the remote onto the bed. "I can't find it. Too many damn channels."

"Ah, sir, Ms. Reed, your manager just arrived. Should I—"

"It's okay, Juan, leave us," Angela Reed said.

Jory rolled his eyes and fell on the bed. Juan hurried out of the room.

"This room is a pigsty," she said. She held up the last bottle of vodka he'd drunk this morning.

"Well, it's my room, and I don't recall inviting you." He shot her a look.

"Jory," she said, walking around and picking up this and that, "I've been trying to reach you for two days. You're not answering your phone. Did you cancel your voice mail? I can't even leave a message anymore."

"There's no one I want to hear from. Listen, I was at the studio yesterday. I'm going through a dry spell."

"You've been drinking," she accused. "Have you spoken to your sponsor? You need to attend a meeting, maybe?"

"Fuck that shit," he said. "I can handle it. I'm not a kid. Now, if you don't mind, I'm missing my show."

"What show?"

"Oh, my husband is talking on early morning television. It's the closest I'll get to him. Maybe I'll jerk off during the

134

show," he sneered.

Angela threw up her hands.

"Listen, just get out, okay? I want to look at Dax, then go to sleep. Don't worry. I'll be back in the studio tomorrow, promise." His voice softened. "I'm a little under the weather. You'll get your damn CD."

"Find your phone, Jory," she advised. "I'll tell them you'll be in the studio tomorrow."

When she left, Jory called to Juan.

He came running in. "Sir?"

"Don't let anyone else in. I'm not here, I'm dead, whatever. Find that show and then close the door and go shopping or something."

Juan found the recording and left. Jory sped through her introduction and the commercial.

"Ladies and gentlemen," Brenda-Lee announced, "please welcome, the one and only, Dax Franklin." And there he was, gorgeous, smiling. He embraced Brenda-lee and took a seat opposite her. The audience was still applauding, hollering, and yelling. He was dressed in blue jeans and a red t-shirt, his hair now to his shoulders, hanging loose. It was hard to take your eyes off Dax.

Even Brenda-lee seemed hypnotized by him. "Yeah, bitch," Jory called out, "you have no idea. If you knew how my husband could kiss, could fuck, you'd be on your knees." He grabbed one of the half-empty bottles and took a swig.

"Dax," she said, "tell us about your decision to leave Intoxication in twenty fifteen."

"I wasn't well. I was addicted to pills, alcohol, and the life I'd been leading was killing me. I had to make a choice."

"At that time, you were still married to Jory Carter."

"That's right."

"You had quite a reputation after you joined the band, you were the bad boy and the sex symbol of the band. That caused problems between you and the late, Luke Wheeler. Can you tell us about that?"

"Luke and the other guys were older, in their thirties, when I came along. We had different ideas. There were some ego problems. But Luke and I mended ways this time."

"We were all sad to hear about Luke. Do you want to tell us about the night he died?"

Jory noticed the look on Dax's face. "Oh, baby," he said softly to the screen. "I wish I could hold you. You're so sad.

"Luke wanted to do this," Dax told the audience. "I think he knew that even after he got surgery for his heart, he wouldn't be able to get back out there. The doctors advised against the tour but there was no stopping Luke. He loved his music, the fans, loved the band he founded. He died the way he wanted to, on stage."

"And you tried to save him."

"Yes. I tried to revive him. It kept him alive until he got to the hospital, but his heart was too damaged. He didn't want to be on life support."

Jory came and sat on the edge of the bed. He hung on Dax's every word, his sincerity and strength coming through as he spoke. "My beautiful baby," Jory whispered, touching the screen. "How I love you and how we've fucked everything all up. What am I doing here without you?"

"And what can fans expect now with you as Intoxications' front man?" Brenda-lee was asking.

"Greatness," Jory whispered out loud. "Dax is the best."

"More of the same," Dax replied with a smile. "We want to pay homage to Luke, sing his songs, and play his music. Doug Lalonde will join us so there will be an extra guitarist on hand."

"You've won countless awards for your guitar playing. It has been said about you that you are one of the greatest rock guitarists ever."

He smiled. "And I appreciate that."

"The talk is that you had no intention of coming back to rock and roll before this reunion tour. What will happen at the end of it? Are your fans to be deprived of your talents?"

"We still have eight months to go," he said.

Jory recognized an evasive answer when he heard one.

Brenda-lee looked at the camera and put up the tour schedule. "Here is the list of cities where you can catch Intoxication. Many of the shows are almost sold out already, so hurry if you want to see a great band." She turned to Dax. "Thank you, Dax, for being here. And I hope that you won't disappear after the tour is finished. Maybe one day you will give us a clear answer about that."

He smiled. "Maybe there isn't one," he said.

The credits rolled, and Dax waved to the camera, then stood and hugged the host.

Jory walked out into the living room. Juan had followed his instructions and fully stocked the bar. He'd finished what was left of the bottle in his room — time to open another.

As Jory sipped the vodka, he looked around for his phone. He was trying to recall the last two days. "Okay," he said, "I left Luke's funeral, waited for Dax, who never bothered to come, and then, oh, yeah," Jory ran into the bathroom. There was his cell phone floating in the bathtub. Had he run a bath?

He picked up the phone. It was dead. "Dead by drowning." He laughed. He threw it back in the water. He'd gone to the studio the next day, but he'd argued with one of the sound techs. Someone chewed him out for being late. He almost hit a pedestrian on the way home, and that was all he remembered.

Fuck it. Fuck them all. He went back into the bedroom and put gay porn on the pay channel. He brought the bottle with him.

He passed out. When he woke up, some muscle-bound guy

was being tied to a bed, and two others were preparing to torture the hell out of him. Jory stumbled out of bed and turned off the television. He was alone. He was lonely. He wanted to go out dancing. That's it. He'd dance.

When he pulled his Trams Am out of the underground parking lot an hour later, he put the peddle to the floor, peeling out into traffic. A roar of horns bellowed at him. He laughed and showed them his finger. "I'm Jory Carter, Jory Carter-Franklin, you losers!" He stopped briefly at a red light, then floored it again.

He turned on the radio, singing along to whatever song came on. Then the announcer said, "Intoxication, leaving Vegas, onto New York City. We have a ticket available, VIP section, for the first caller who can tell us the name of this song."

The song was one of Dax's from way back when Jory used to fantasize about the posters on his wall. When Dax started to sing, Jory punched the steering wheel. "Love me long," he whispered. "Song is called *Love Me Long*." He started to sing. "All night, love me long, for tomorrow I'll be gone." He pounded the steering wheel again, taking the corner on two wheels.

He parked in the middle of the street, hollering to the parking valet. "Park it!" He threw the keys at him and walked into the night club, the same kind of night club where he and Dax had first met in New York years ago.

Many people greeted him, some he knew, some not. He went up to the bar, ordered a vodka, and started to dance. He was having a great time until he wasn't. The people in front of him became nothing but a blur. Someone touched his arm. He lashed out, hit someone. He wasn't sure who. He headed to the bathroom. He was sitting on the floor when someone came in and picked him up.

After that, he remembered nothing. When he opened his

eyes, he wasn't sure where he was. The sunlight was streaming through the windows, and the room he was in was luxurious. He tried to sit up, but his head was pounding.

The door opened, and someone he recognized stood there.

"Elly?" he said. It was Luke's daughter.

"Hey there," she said, coming over to the bed. "How are you doing?"

"Headache. What, how did I get here?"

She smiled. "Someone told me you were at Club Throb last night, and ah, you passed out in the men's. I had you brought here. I didn't want you to drive. I thought you'd gone through the rehab thing and that you were on the wagon?"

"You know, I appreciate what you did, Elly, but please, I don't need a lecture."

"Okay. It's just I've seen it a lot growing up with the band. You weren't drinking at Dad's service."

"No."

"Is this because you and Dax talked, and it didn't work out? I mean, it's not my business or anything."

He just stared at her. "You mean after we talked here?"

"No, I mean when he went to your house."

"He didn't come to my house. I waited and waited, and he didn't come." Jory rubbed his eyes.

"He said he was going. It was super early. The sun was up. I kept him with me. And if you want the truth, I tried to seduce him."

Jory's eyes widened.

"Don't worry. He turned me down flat. Then I remembered. I wasn't trying to keep your message from him, but maybe I wanted to delay it. I'm sorry. I should have told him right after you left. I needed him. I didn't want to be alone."

Jory was speechless.

"He had your number, too," she continued. "I'm surprised he didn't try calling. He said he really wanted to talk to you."

"Shit." Jory sat up. "I got drunk. I must have passed out. I didn't hear the bell. And I threw my phone in the bathtub."

She laughed. "Why?"

"I don't know. Damn. Can I get hold of him? He doesn't have the same number, does he? I know he changes it often when he's on tour."

"He sent me a text this morning," Elly said, showing Jory her phone. "Short and sweet but that's Dax."

Hey, Cookie Girl. Everything is cool. Thanks for the pictures of your dad as a kid, we are adding them to the presentation on the screen at the shows. Heading to the Big Apple. Everyone sends love. Xxx

"I'll copy down the number for you. Why don't you go to New York and meet up with him?" she asked.

"Like this? No." Jory put his face in his hands. "I never thought I'd have to say this again. I need to go back to rehab."

Elly sat beside him and hugged him. "You'll do it for real this time but, Jory, you need to be with Dax. Find a way."

"It's hard, Elly. You see, I don't think I want this life anymore."

"Really?"

He nodded. "And now Dax is getting the bug again."

"He's doing it for Dad. I think he's quite disenchanted with the life, Jory. I doubt he's going to continue with the band. I really do think this is the end of it."

"You know, you probably saved me from killing someone, or myself last night." He kissed her cheek.

She smiled. "The least I could do. All the time you spent playing with me when you could have been making love with Dax. It was quite the sacrifice." She laughed.

Jory grinned. "It sure was."

"So, how is he really?" she whispered. "In the sack?"

Jory lifted his eyebrows and smiled. "Oh, baby."

She swatted him. "Hate you. Now get your act together, please."

"Can I borrow your phone? I need to call my sponsor."

She handed him her phone. "And text Dax. Tell him the truth."

Jory took a breath. "Right now, I don't want him to know." He eyed her. "And don't you tell him."

"But he'd want to know, Jory," Elly insisted.

"Dax has enough on his shoulders right now."

She smiled. "But he has broad shoulders and a beautiful—"

"Hey." Jory pointed at her, hiding a smile. "I let you get away with trying to seduce my husband. Don't push your luck."

She laughed. "I saw him naked once when I was a kid. He was coming out of the shower. It's a hard thing to get out of your mind."

"I know what you mean," Jory agreed. "How come you were spying on my man in the shower anyway?"

"Wasn't. The shower in his room was broken, so he asked to borrow Dad's. It was just timing. Lucky for me, but I was too young to fully appreciate it."

"Tough luck," Jory told her. "Okay, I need to make some calls."

"I'll give you some privacy."

"Elly, really." He looked at her. "Thank you."

She nodded and left the room.

After getting off the phone with his sponsor, he found himself thinking about Dax. Were they even still married? The papers were signed. What did that mean? Damn you, Ben, he thought. How could I have ever trusted that guy?

His sponsor called back twenty minutes later. He was making the arrangements for rehab. "It should be in-patient this time, Jory," he said.

"Okay."

"Tell me where to pick you up. I'm coming right away.

We'll talk when I get there."

"I'm at Luke's mansion in Beverly Hills."

"Luke, as in the Intoxication?"

"Yes."

"What are you doing there?"

"Long story." Jory reminded him of the address and hung up.

When he said goodbye to Elly, he said, "When you hear from Dax, don't tell him I'm in rehab.

When I'm well, I will find him. Okay?"

"Are you sure about this? What if Dax is trying to find you and he asks me if I've seen you?"

"You didn't." He kissed her cheek. "I need to do this alone, and it will be the last time because I'm working for the greatest reward of all, and it's not my career."

She hugged him. "You tell me where you are. I'll visit you."

Jory smiled and nodded.

He was ready when Paul Deluca arrived. In the car, Paul explained about the Center Jory was headed to. "It's a good place in New Mexico. Discrete. They are used to dealing with celebrities."

Jory didn't say anything. He just sat quietly in the back of the vehicle. "Can you get me a cell phone, Paul? I need to call my manager."

"Of course, let her know things are on hold."

"No," Jory shook his head, "let her know that whatever it costs; I want out of my contract."

"Are you sure, Jory?" Paul looked at him. "That's a lot to give up.

"I have already given up the one thing that matters most. I know now how meaningless this is. The fans, the money, the fancy cars, and parties. I don't care about any of those things."

"You may change your mind, Jory. You're not thinking clearly right now," Paul explained.

"Even though I really want a drink right now, my mind has never been clearer. This time, I'm making a new start. All the signs were there in New York, and I blew it. My ego got in the way, dollar signs and stars in front of my eyes. But it's not that I want. And drinking myself to death will never fill the void."

"So, if you don't want your career, what do you want?" He looked at him.

"Dax Franklin." He met Paul's gaze.

Paul's eyes widened. "That's it?" He laughed. "You can't live on loving Dax Franklin."

"You've never loved Dax Franklin." Jory smirked. "To start, yes, that's it, I need to be with the love of my life, the only man I'll ever truly want. Together, we'll figure things out."

"And what if it doesn't work out with you and Dax? That could jeopardize your sobriety. I wouldn't put all your hopes on Dax."

"Dax is my life. I need to get my life back, Paul." He swallowed. "I'll get on my knees, I'll beg him. After my treatment, I'm going to give him the best me I can. I know that deep in his heart, he still loves me. And that will carry me through the treatment."

CHAPTER ELEVEN

They were all there on stage for the final number, Reggie, Jack, and even Doug Lalonde, and Hank Monroe. In the background were flashes of Luke Wheeler and the original band.

It was emotional for all of them. They all knew that something important was ending.

When it was over, Dax stood there on stage with the rest of the band, feeling drained and sad. They bowed to the audience, then left the stage. In the dressing room, they sat together. No one spoke for a long time. Finally, Reggie got to his feet and raised up a bottle of something. "To Luke," he said.

The others echoed his words. Dax downed some water.

Reggie looked over at Dax. Then Jack stood up as well. "Dax," Reggie announced, "I know we've had our differences, but none of those things mean anything now. Jack and I, well." Reggie turned to Jack for help as emotion claimed his voice.

Jack cleared his throat. "We know you didn't want to come back to the band, but we couldn't have done this without you. The shows were sold out because the fans wouldn't have accepted anyone but you in Luke's shoes. You gave everything up on that stage, blood and sweat and tears. You truly are the best."

Dax nodded. "Thanks."

"And Luke knew that," Reggie added. "So, that's why I'm going to donate the money I earned on this tour to help drug addicts and alcoholics, and something else." He took a breath. "That talk we had a few months back, Dax, you were right. I'm going to do it for real this time. No bullshit."

Dax had told Reggie he needed to go back to rehab. He was happy to know he'd listened and truly humbled by what his bandmates said.

They hugged each other and Jack said, "I'm donating mine, too. Maybe you can tell me where it should go, okay?"

Dax smiled. "We'll do it together."

"So, now what?" Reggie asked Dax. "Are you going back to Canada?"

"Yes. I have the nightclub and some good friends there." He smiled. "What about you, guys?"

"I'm going to be incognito for a few months," Reggie said.

Dax smiled. "Look me up when you're out."

Reggie nodded.

Jack looked at Dax. "Now that it's legal in Canada, maybe I'll do a bit of farming over there. You think you can help me to immigrate?"

Dax laughed. "I'll do what I can to help."

"You are coming to the party," Jack insisted. "I know you usually go off alone, but it's kind of special tonight."

"I'll be there," Dax told them.

The party was at the Beverly Hills Hotel, by invitation only. The band arrived in a limo, along with Doug and Hank. The media went crazy when they got out of the vehicle. Police and security kept the screaming fans at bay. Dax knew he wouldn't miss this at all.

It took at least twenty minutes to get inside and whisked into one of the main ballrooms. There were champagne fountains and more cameras flashing, television commentators, and celebrities. Dax was greeted by so many people his head was spinning.

Then he saw a familiar face, and he felt the stress drain from his body. She looked wonderful in a sparkling, silver gown. Elly stood with her in a short blue party dress. They both waved at him. Dax ignored people in the crowd and hurried toward them. "Freda!" He hugged her and kissed her. "I've missed you so much. Why didn't you tell me you were coming?"

"I didn't know," she said. "This is Elly's doing. She got me in here. Pretty exclusive."

Dax kissed Elly on the cheek and hugged her. "Hello, girl, thanks for bringing Freda. I didn't know you two had gotten so chummy."

"When she came to Vancouver" — Freda took Elly's arm — "we had a girl to girl talk one afternoon."

Elly smiled. "And I got some damn good advice."

Elly had broken it off with Reggie then. He hadn't realized that Freda had had a hand in that.

"The show was incredible, sweetie," Freda said. "You were so good and the guys. What a show!"

Elly hugged Dax's arm. "My dad was watching and smiling. Thanks, Dax."

He grinned. "You're welcome."

"You are coming home, aren't you, darling?" Freda asked him. "Everyone misses you, especially me. And I need you at the club. I've held off on booking more live bands until you come home. You are so much better at picking them than I am."

They were both looking at him, waiting for an answer.

"Yes, I'm coming home. Of course." Some people came over to speak to him, take pictures.

Freda moved up close and whispered in his ear, "I have something to tell you."

He looked at her.

A reporter came up and snapped their picture together.

"So, who is this, Dax, a new love interest?"

Dax put his arm around her. "Yes, love, love for my best friend in the entire world, my rock, and my business partner from Canada." He kissed Freda again.

Another reporter began to ask Freda questions. Elly grabbed Dax's hand and pulled him closer. "Come dance with me."

That was the last thing he felt like doing, but if it got him away from the reporters, that was great. It was slow, so Dax took Elly in his arms, and they swayed to a tune that was difficult to follow with all the noise. "How are you doing?" he asked her.

"I'm fine," she said. "I'm going to take things slow. I'm thinking about moving out your way."

"Really? That's nice," Dax said.

"Freda offered me a job at the club. Would you mind?" She looked up at him.

"I'd love it," he said.

"Dax?"

"Um?" he asked, smiling and nodding to some people who crossed their path.

"What?"

"It's about what Freda wanted to tell you." The song ended, and they broke apart.

"About what?" Dax asked.

"Jory." She seemed to hold her breath.

"I tried to see him months ago, Elly. He didn't want to talk to me. What do you want me to do?"

"He went back to rehab," she told him.

Dax's eyes widened. "What? When? What happened? Why didn't someone tell me?"

"He wanted to do it on his own." She grabbed his arm. "And he has, Dax. He's sober. Been that way for two months now."

"Good." Tears came to his eyes. "Damn. I should have been there for him. I could have helped him. I—"

"Dax. He loves you so much. He wanted to be healthy when he came to you. "

Dax shook his head. "Came to me?"

"He wants to be with you. I know you've been too busy, and you don't read the entertainment stuff, but he doesn't want to perform anymore. He's out of his contract."

Dax opened his mouth to speak. He was in shock.

"He didn't do it for you," she said. "It's what he truly wants."

"He's out of rehab? Where is he?"

"Yes. He's out."

"Where is he? Is he here in LA?"

"He was. He was in the audience tonight. He wanted to be there for your last show. He loved it. We all did. We even shed some tears."

Someone was speaking to him. Dax waved them away. He was still staring at Elly. "He was in the audience. Where is he now?"

"He left right after to show to go home. He had something he needed to do."

"Home where? Why all the mystery? I need to speak to him. He didn't want to see me?"

"You still love him, don't you Dax?" She appeared to be holding her breath.

"Yes, of course, I still love him." Dax swallowed.

"Then be patient." She smiled and walked away.

Dax was perplexed. He searched all over for Freda, but she was nowhere to be found. Finally, Elly disappeared, too. He ended up spending some more time with the guys in the band, and then they all went their separate ways, promising to keep in touch.

Dax was exhausted, and despite all this confusion about

Jory, he fell asleep as soon as he got to his room, with all his clothes on.

When he finally woke up, it was the next evening. He called Freda. He needed answers.

"Hello, rock star," she teased.

"Yeah, yeah," he told her. "Okay, what's going on? Why didn't you tell me Jory was in rehab again and where is he now? Why didn't he come to the reception last night?"

"I know nothing. Just come home, sweetie, and try not to worry." She hung up.

"Damn it all!" Dax got up, took a shower. He tried to call Elly, got her voice mail. He called Freda again, no answer. He called the Club in Vancouver. He got Bryan. "The FreDax. My name is Bryan. How may I help you?"

"Bryan, it's Dax." He could hear the music blaring in the background.

"Oh, hello, boss. We've missed you. When are you coming home?"

"Soon. Do you know where Freda is? Is she there?"

"Freda who?"

"Bryan!"

"Oh, yes, that Freda. Not at the moment. Ah, she went for a . . . a manicure."

"It's nine o'clock at night. And Elly, where is she?"

"She went, too. There's this all-night place. New. A Girl thing."

"Right. Bullshit. Okay, fine." He sighed. "I'll be in tomorrow. Can you let Freda know?"

"Okay, text her the time. Bye." The phone went dead.

Dax stared at the receiver. This was just weird. And where was Jory? Why hadn't he stayed last night? Why all the mystery?

CHAPTER TWELVE

"This has not been easy. Dax is not a man who likes intrigue, and he was mighty curious about why you didn't hang around last night," Freda scolded Jory.

"It just wasn't the place to do this," Jory said. "It has to be perfect. Is everything ready for tomorrow?"

Freda sat down beside him on the sofa and put her arm around him. Jory put his head on her shoulder. She stroked his hair. "You need to go to sleep. You don't want to greet Dax tomorrow with big black circles under your eyes, do you?"

"I can't sleep." He looked at her. "What if he says no?"

"I will beat the living crap out of that boy," she said. "And don't let the high heels fool you, baby."

Jory laughed. "Please don't. I need him in one piece."

"I won't hurt the important parts." She winked. "Stop stressing. You know what Elly told you."

"Yes, he said he still loves me, but what if it's like a brother?"

Freda shook her head. "Are we talking about the same Dax? Why in the world would Dax not want to ravish that fine ass of yours? You forget his reputation. That boy might not want the rock star life anymore, but he's still a bad boy deep down."

Jory smiled. He liked the sound of that.

Freda gave him a shove off the sofa. "Now get that fine ass of yours into the bedroom. Sleep because, darling, if I know my Dax, you're going to need all your energy for reunion sex."

Jory stood, looking at her. "Do you think he had sex when he was on tour?"

"Oh, baby," she said. "I don't know. Does that matter? He'll be yours for the rest of your life. You don't expect him to be a monk, do you? And the divorce was final."

"He could use his hand," Jory muttered.

"You just imagine that's what he did, if it makes you feel better." Freda made a face and pushed him down the hall. "Now, sleep. I'm going to the club for a look-see, and then I'm coming back. I have to pick up Dax at the airport tomorrow."

"Shit, I have so much to do." Jory moaned.

"Now, sleep, you will have plenty of time tomorrow," she insisted, shoving him into the bedroom and closing the door.

Jory paced. How could he sleep? His entire future rested on seeing Dax tomorrow. He went to the bureau and took out the little box. A new ring, a new proposal, they'd be starting all over. "Dax," he whispered, "please, marry me again. This time we won't fuck it up." He closed the box and put it back in the drawer.

He went to lay down on the bed, but there was no way he was going to fall asleep. These last few months without Dax had been hell. Jory was so proud of him, doing what he did for Luke Wheeler, letting Luke go out in a blaze of glory. And he'd done it all sober, without falling back into the bottle.

Rehab had been harder this time, but he'd kept at it. He told his therapist, "I never really wanted to be famous. I enjoyed the perks that went along with it. All I've ever wanted was to be with Dax Franklin. From the moment we met, he has been the center of my universe. I will find out what I want to do with my life but with him beside me."

Elly had come to see him in rehab as promised, and one day, she brought a friend. It was Freda. She was gorgeous and gregarious, and everything Dax said she'd be. When Elly left them to talk, Freda leaned over and looked Jory in the eye.

"You listen, boy, you break Dax's heart one more time, and you will deal with me. Do you understand?"

Jory nodded, smiling. "Yes," he said. "I'm happy Dax has you in his life. He spoke of you often when he was in New York. He loves you a lot."

"We are in each other's lives, baby. And I love him, too. He gave me hope when there was none, taught me to love myself again. What do you want, Jory? Tell me."

"Dax. I want Dax. I don't want to run around the world anymore. I want to wake up beside him every morning, make love to him every night. We belong together."

"You won't blame him for giving up your career?" She waited. "It's his worst fear."

"No. He gave me fame. It was a gift, and I loved it, but after a while, I realized that it's not the life for me. I had to come this far on this journey to figure it all out."

Freda stood. "The most important lessons are the hardest," she said. "Get well and hightail your ass out to Vancouver, boy. On your knees, boy, and beg if you have to because Dax is the real deal."

"I know he is. I got a lot to make up for. So, is that an invite?" He smiled at her.

"You know how to wait a table?" She eyed him.

"Sure do."

"Okay, call me. Elly will give you my number. Be well, sweetie." She kissed his cheek.

And here he was in Vancouver. He'd been here over a month, and Freda had mothered him like he was a lost puppy. Elly was here now too. The only thing missing was Dax, and then life would be just about perfect.

Dax was on his way. This was the day he'd been waiting for. In the dark, he said, "I promise all the powers that be I will love him and cherish him until my last breath. Please bring him back to me."

When he finally went to sleep, he dreamt of a time when he and Dax had been together. It was shortly after they got married and they went away for a few weeks, a quiet cabin on an Island. There were no cameras, no reporters. They walked in the woods, swam in the ocean, ate, and made love. He could see Dax on the beach now, shirtless, his long hair blowing gently in the breeze. Above them, the moon shone down, and Jory watched Dax come out of the water, droplets of water on his bronze skin. He was laughing about something, speaking words Jory couldn't hear. All he could do was look at him, helpless in his power, anticipating the seconds it would take Dax to cross the sand and sit down beside him, take him into his arms.

I want to touch you. I want to lick the water from your skin and crawl inside you. God, how could I ever let you go, Dax? Kiss me. Let's stay here forever.

"Dax?" Jory's eyes opened. He could almost feel him there beside him. He snaked his hand down to his cock, wet and sticky. He'd come in his sleep like a damn teenager. Jory got out of bed, went into the bathroom, and cleaned up. "I'm seventeen again," he said to his image in the mirror. "Dax, you prick." He smiled.

Freda came out into the hallway, dressed in her bathrobe. "You okay, Angel? I heard you cry out in your sleep."

"I'm fine." He smiled. "A dream."

She didn't comment, just turned around and went back to her room. It seemed to take forever for morning to come. When Freda got up, Jory gave her a cup of coffee and asked her what time she was going to pick Dax up.

She grinned. "He gets in later this afternoon. Did you sleep, honey?"

"Not much. Did you check to see what flight he left on? Is it on time? It wasn't delayed, was it? He's on the plane, right?"

"Do you want me to text him?" She lifted an eyebrow, grinning.

Jory nodded. "Sure."

Smiling, Freda picked up her phone.

"I know I'm being a pest."

"I think it's cute." Freda was tapping away on her phone. She looked at him. "He's flying direct. Takes around three hours. He hasn't left for the airport yet. His flight leaves at two this afternoon."

"So that would get him to the airport at around supper time?" Jory sipped his coffee.

Freda nodded at him while she was reading. She laughed.

"What?"

"He wants to know what is wrong with Bryan." Freda giggled. "Asking me now if I went for a manicure with Elly last night." She looked at Jory. "Couldn't Bryan have come up with a better reason than a manicure? Makes no sense. Dax may not know much about girlie things, but he does know I don't go for a manicure in the evening."

Jory laughed out loud.

Freda shut down the phone. "Anyway, I told Dax I'd be there to pick him up. He says he is anxious to come home."

"Good." Jory sucked in some air. "I want everything to be perfect when you bring him to the club tonight."

"It will be, boy. Now, for God's sakes calm down and let's eat something before I faint from hunger."

CHAPTER THIRTEEN

Dax was anxious to get off the plane. He was in first class, which was comfortable, but his plan to get some sleep on the plane was only wishful thinking. Many people wanted to speak to him, to tell him they'd seen one of the concerts and how they enjoyed it. They asked him about his future, talked about Luke, and he ended up signing a couple of autographs.

When the steward asked him if he'd like her to tell the passengers not to bother him, he shrugged. "It's okay," he said. "I don't mind." It took his mind off things, Jory, mainly. He was worried. Jory in rehab again and he hadn't even told him. This morning he thought about the divorce. Jory didn't owe him an explanation anymore now that the divorce was final. But still. It pained him to think that Jory had started to drink again.

So, he ended up chatting to several people about music and the band, and the flight didn't seem so long anymore. By the time they touched down in Vancouver, he felt sleepy. When he stood up to get off, there was a round of applause and some whistles. He turned around and nodded his thanks.

In the airport, he went through customs and headed for the luggage rack. He had just picked up his suitcase when he spotted Freda walking in his direction. It was spring now, and she was all about flowers in her knee-length floral tunic and pink leggings. She was wearing flats which put them at about the same height.

They embraced, and she stood back looking at him. "Honey, what are you wearing?"

He had on a pair of designer jeans. They'd cost him a fortune with all the rips in the right places. He had pulled on the blue t-shirt from the Intoxication tour and wore white runners.

"Why?" Dax wrinkled his nose. Freda was the fashion police.

"Those jeans." She pulled at them. "They're too big."

"I've lost some weight."

"Are you sure they didn't come from one of those poor houses?"

"Try Chez Dan, tailor-made for me at four big ones," he told her

"Four dollars, I'd believe," she protested.

"Four thousand dollars," he countered, making a face.

"Honey, you got taken. And what kind of tailor was that?"

"I lost twenty pounds on the road, and I only gained back five. So, they're loose. And don't say anything about my t-shirt." He pointed at her.

"You brought me one, I hope."

"Of course," he said, laughing.

"Looks faded. What was written on the back?"

"Kiss my ass," he told her with a straight face.

"I'm not sure how to take that," she replied, then punched his arm. "But the shadow thing is hot, better than the beard, and your hair"—she reached around and grabbed the ponytail—"long. Did you streak it?"

They began walking to the door. "No. I didn't streak it. Don't get any ideas. And why all this concern about my appearance?"

She shrugged. "Darling, you're gorgeous. Just want you to show it off."

He grabbed her hand and studied her nails. "Looks like you're due for a manicure." He eyed her. They stopped outside. He put a hand on her arm. "What's going on?"

"It's going to rain." She pointed at the sky.

"There's not a cloud up there. Freda?" He met her gaze.

She wasn't looking at him. Suddenly, she said, "Oh my God, I'm illegally parked. They will tow my ass. Come on, rock star."

Freda ran across the parking lot. Dax hurried after her. He watched her open the trunk for his suitcases. "You're not illegally —"

"Get in," she said, closing the trunk after he'd put his cases in. She threw him the keys. "You drive."

"Okay." Dax got behind the wheel and rolled out of the parking space. When they were on the road, Dax looked at her and said, "You're not a good liar, my friend."

"Lovely day," she announced

"Thought you said it was going to rain?" Dax raised an eyebrow.

"What are you, the weather police? I said it looked like rain a while ago but not now."

"A while ago was like ten minutes. Freda, where is Jory? Why were you with him at the concert? And why didn't Jory come to see me after the show?"

"He was busy."

"How do you know him?"

"You were married to him," she said

"Yes, but you never met him. Did Elly introduce you?" Dax glanced at her.

"Yes."

"And where is he now?"

"Stop it, Dax. We have no time for your trivial questions. You need to get home, take a shower, and get dressed."

"For what?" he asked. "My plan is to unpack, order in, and watch some movie on the tube, then fall asleep. I don't have to dress up for that."

"I bought you a new shirt. I want you to wear it with those

blue leather pants, the navy ones. The shirt I bought is a sky blue. Beautiful."

"It's not my birthday, why did you buy me a shirt?" he asked, looking at her.

"Oh damn, I forgot, well early birthday present."

"And those blue leather pants don't fit anymore. They are too small."

"You said you lost weight. They'll fit. Now shut up and drive already. I want to get home in one piece, and slow down."

Dax chuckled. "Okay. So, at least tell me what I have to dress up for?"

"The Club. The staff at the club have missed you, and they are planning a little coming home party before we open. So, you need to dress up." Freda rummaged in her purse for her phone. She was busy tapping away while Dax drove.

Dax wrinkled his nose. "I don't want any —"

"What are you doing, honey?" Freda demanded as he drove up in front of the club. "We need to go to your place."

"Why? Are you going to dress me?" He laughed. "Mommy, I can dress myself."

"Don't be a smart ass." She whacked him.

"Ouch."

"Just take me to your place, okay. We'll go to the club together."

"I'm starving. Do I get to eat?"

"Not until we are sure those pants fit. Damn, I picked the shirt specifically to go with them."

Dax grumbled and rolled his eyes.

"Now, hurry up."

When Dax pulled into his driveway, Freda hopped out of the car. As Dax walked up to his front door and put the key in the lock, he noticed that Freda was crying.

"What's wrong?" he asked.

"Nothing, I'm happy. Get your ass inside and in the shower." She shoved him inside. "I had someone water your plants."

"Great," he said, putting down his luggage.

"Go on," she said, pushing him. "Leave the shadow and where's your blow dryer?"

"Ah, God knows, I never use it."

Freda began taking products out of the oversized bag she carried around.

Dax made a face. "What are those for?"

"Never mind, go, before I rip those Salvation Army clothes off your back." She swatted Dax on the butt.

"I'm going. I'm going. What the hell?"

Whatever bug bit Freda, it was a determined one. Dax got in the shower, letting the powerful spray do its magic. He soaped up, washed his hair, and stood there, enjoying the way the water cascaded over him, soothing his aching muscles. He would have preferred to stay home. He was tired but there was no arguing with Freda when she got like this.

Suddenly the glass door slid open and Freda stood there, towel in hand.

"Ah," Dax let out a shout. "You scared the shit out of me. Do you mind?"

Freda stood back and looked him over. "Damn, boy, you're enough to make this poor girl cream her panties."

"Give me that," he told her, yanking the towel out of her hands. "Pervert. And what is the damn hurry?"

"We should be there now. Come on." She ran her hands over his face. "Perfect, don't touch it. Where's your brush? Never mind, I have one. Let's get you into those clothes and do your hair."

"Freda," he protested.

She held out the blue leather pants. He'd bought those pants when he'd been with the band. He was sure they wouldn't fit. "No underwear," she said. "Are you dry?"

"Would you like to see?"

"Ha, ha. You don't need diapers yet. Put them on. Watch the jewels." She smiled.

"Funny." He pulled them on. "Tight fit. I haven't worn these since I was eighteen years old."

"Suck it in," she said, watching as he pulled up the zipper. She turned him around. "Look at that ass. My God, holy, holy. Okay, the shirt." She handed him a very expensive blue shirt.

"Freda, this is really nice. Thank you." He slipped the shirt on and began to do it up. As he finished putting on the shirt, he heard the sound of a hairdryer.

"Your welcome, get over here, sit, I'm going to dry all that hair of yours."

"Don't put anything stinky in it," he warned her.

"Okay, I won't." After his hair was dry, she told him to put on his boots.

She was texting when he came out into the living room. She stopped and looked at him. "There's my Dax. Beautiful. Okay, stud, let's go. We're late already. You can't be late."

Freda drove, and Dax had never seen her drive so fast. She pulled into the club on two wheels. "Ah Freda, why is the parking lot full of cars at this time of night?"

She shrugged. "Don't know."

They got out, and Dax headed to the front door. "I know you *do* know."

"No, no," she said, taking his arm and dragging him around back.

"Freda! What the hell are you doing?"

"Front door is broken," she said, pulling him inside the back door.

"Broken? Well, let me see if I can fix—"

"No, no." She pulled him down the hallway, looking around. "I'll call a handyman."

Elly appeared, all dressed up in a long yellow dress.

"Thank heavens, take him, Elly," Freda said. "I have to get dressed."

Elly took his arm. Dax looked her over. "What's going on? Why are you dressed like that?"

"What, you don't like it?" She held his arm tightly.

"You look like you're going to a —"

"No, no, not at all. Going nowhere, really. Don't be difficult."

Dax moved forward. "Difficult? I'm not being difficult."

"Where are you going now?" she asked, holding onto his arm.

"Why are we standing here in the hallway? I want to say hello to the staff." He tried to move forward again, but she held onto him.

"Elly?" He pulled his arm away.

Bryan appeared. He smiled. "Hey, boss." He looked at Elly. "Ready."

"Thank God," she said. "He's being difficult."

Dax just stared at her.

"Come on." She pulled him forward, then walked him through the door to the main room. It was dark.

"What's wrong with the electricity?"

He heard a note from the piano. A spotlight came on, then the first chords of music. He recognized them right away. It was the first song he and Jory ever wrote together. Jory sang him the words in the park that night. Later, Dax had written the music. Now, Jory began singing those words again.

Love waits to spin me round and round. I can't wait to leave the ground. Are you the one to take me on the wind? Take me on the wind, I never want to land. Lay me in the sand and be my love.

As he stood there listening, he held back tears. His throat was all choked up. Freda appeared beside him, taking his other arm. He gave her a questioning look. She just smiled.

The song ended. Although Dax could sense people all

around, there was no sound. Suddenly Jory stood. He was dressed in a dark suit, white shirt. He looked incredible. He had the microphone and he came down off the stage. He stood in the middle of the floor.

Dax wasn't sure what to do.

"Dax," Jory said, his voice sounding shaky. "I'm here tonight to ask you one question, and if the answer is yes, come out here and stand with me. If it's no, then you won't walk out here to meet me. It will break my heart in two, but it has to be your choice. Over these last few years, I have lived a life some people can only dream of. And all of that is because you had faith in me, you fought for me. I'd never have had any of what I had without you. But the thing is, I came to realize that it was all meaningless. When I woke up in the morning, you weren't beside me. When I closed my eyes at night, I'd reach for you, and you weren't there. I've had my taste of fame. Now, I'm full of that. But I could never be full of you. I'll love you and want you forever. That's why" — his voice broke and he went down on one knee, opening the ring box and holding it out—"I'm asking you to marry me," he paused and said, "again."

There wasn't a dry eye in the club, including the two ladies on his arms. Dax kissed Freda and Elly, then walked out into the middle of the floor. He stood there looking down at him, then reached out and took his hand, bringing Jory to his feet. "Yes," he said softly, "yes, and yes." He smiled as the tears ran down Jory's face.

There was applause as Jory reached up and touched his cheek. Dax leaned in and kissed him. Then Jory put the ring on Dax's finger. Dax smiled, noticing that Jory still wore his. Jory moved away from him and blew him a kiss.

Dax looked around as Freda and Ely took his arm on both sides. Jory waited a few feet away, and then Dax saw another person standing there, a judge in a long black robe. One of

Dax's songs began to play as the two ladies walked him up to where Jory waited.

Senses overflowing, love so demanding. Being with you always, in my heart. Although we said goodbye, I know until I die, our love will be . . . senses overflowing, love so demanding, even in my dreams, I touch your skin . . . so love me now while I'm here and remember when I'm gone. I will always love you."

As Freda and Elly released him to stand beside Jory, Freda said to Jory, "Remember what I told you."

"I'll never break his heart," Jory replied but he was looking at Dax.

"Okay," she said, kissing his cheek. In his ear, she whispered something, and Jory laughed.

Dax took Jory's hand as one of Dax's extended guitar solos played in the background. "You don't waste much time."

"I figured if you said yes." Jory smiled. "I wasn't going to let you change your mind."

The judge said the words. Dax said, yes, to everything. Why wouldn't he? Maybe this time they'd do it right, without the cameras and the fame — just them.

As they cut the cake later, Dax asked Jory what Freda had said to him earlier in his ear.

He laughed. "The pants. She is especially impressed with the way your ass looks in them."

"And you? Are you impressed, too?" He teased.

"Seriously" — Jory picked up a piece of cake and smeared it all over Dax's face — "I can't wait to get you out of them."

YOU MAY ALSO ENJOY THE FOLLOWING FROM eXTASY BOOKS INC:

Blood Pond
D.J. Manly

Excerpt

August opened his laptop in an internet café. He checked his email, relieved to see that finally the money from his last job had been deposited into his PayPal account. He transferred it immediately, aware it would take at least three days before he could access it at a bank machine.

He brought up the Google map and located the gay village. The last time he'd traced Monkton here, he'd just left a job at some strip club on Ste. Catherine Street. The owner of the club had been livid when August had shown him his picture. "The guy wrecked my club, went nuts one night after closing and broke a lot of stuff, left me with over two thousand bucks in damages. He was a drunk, couldn't control his drinking, and fucking crazy. Damn shame though. The clients loved him."

The map reminded him of where this place was. He googled Le Spot, and according to the website, it was still there. So were the owners, Stephen and Karl. He had no reason to think Bruce went back there after what he'd done except that he was an illegal. Chances were that he'd end up dancing in one of these places again for cash. So, if he wasn't at Le Spot, maybe these guys could point him in the right direction.

He finished his coffee, ordered a muffin to go, and found his car again; five blocks down. Damn hard to find parking in this city. He was tempted to take the Metro.

Driving down Ste. Catherine Street was slow and laborious. It was seven o'clock on a Thursday night, and the stores were open until nine. Jaywalking seemed to be perfected to an art in this city. He ate his muffin as he drove and opened his window a crack, watching the swarm of people everywhere.

When he saw the rainbow flag, he looked for parking and luckily found a tight spot on a side street. He got out, pulled his jacket around him, and walked back up to the main drag. The restaurants were full, and so were the stores. Bookstores and sex shops featuring gay erotica in the windows gave people pause as they strolled along.

August checked for the bar at every corner, remembering that it had been upstairs on the second floor, a little out-of-the-way place that was packed the night he visited.

He passed it twice, realizing that they'd changed the sign from white to purple and the fonts on the lettering were fancier. He paused at the bottom as two men brushed past him. They looked back at him and smiled. "Hey, baby," one said. "Aren't you sweet."

Sweet? He'd never been called that before. He nodded at them, and one of the guys held open the door.

"Don't be shy." One man gave him a wink.

August laughed. "Okay," he said and followed him in.

"What's your name?" the guy asked as the other guy wandered off. He was a slim fellow, probably around thirty years old, nice looking.

"August." He smiled. It seemed so far away, even the thought of flirting with someone again.

"This must be my lucky night, August. You're gorgeous.

Can I buy you a drink?"

"Maybe later." Right now, he had more important things to take care of.

He looked around the room as he walked in. It was already half full. August spotted that Stephen guy near the bar and walked over. "Mr. Lachance?"

Stephen Lachance turned around, a tall, well-built Jamaican man with a beautiful, rich accent. He narrowed his eyes, then smiled. "Oui?"

"I don't know if you remember me but—"

"Cheri," he ran his gaze over August, "I'd have to be blind not to remember a man as good-looking as you. What can I help you with?"

"I wanted to ask about someone who worked for you a while back. I believe he went by the name of Clay. I have reason to believe he may be back in Montreal."

"Clay?" He snorted. "Not in my place, he isn't. The guy is a headcase. Loco." He made a circle with his finger round his temple.

"Any idea who may be hiring dancers in the village without . . . well . . ."

"Illegals? Ha, take your pick, baby. They all do it."

"Can you maybe suggest where to start?"

"Come here." He motioned and led him over to the bar. "Relax, sit down, have a drink, on the house." He poured him a whiskey. "You look stressed right out." August thanked him and took a swig.

"Whatever obsession you got with this guy, give it up man. It's going to kill you. He's cute and all but—"

"It's not like that," August told him.

"I've heard that before, sweet man. But if you haven't found him in all this time, he doesn't want to be found. And you can't reform 'em, honey, I know."

"I don't want to reform him," he replied impatiently. "I don't want to fuck him either. I just need him to tell me who murdered my brother."

Stephen Lachance's eyes bugged out of his head.

August drained his glass and put it back down on the bar. He hadn't realized that his voice had gotten so loud. People looked over at the bar curiously. He stood and lowered his voice. His hand shook. "I'm sorry. Look, if you don't want to help me, then don't. Even if it takes fifty fucking years, I'll find him."

He was halfway down the stairs when Stephen Lachance caught up to him. He grabbed his arm and looked him in the eye. "Give me a number where I can reach you.

If I see him, I'll call you, okay?"

August pulled out one of his business cards. "It's my cell phone. Don't worry if I don't answer; leave a message."

He nodded, looking at the card. "Okay. Try to relax, man."

"I'll relax," he said, running down the stairs, "when I find Bruce Monkton."

ABOUT THE AUTHOR

I write not only for my own pleasure but for the pleasure of my readers. I can't remember a time in my life when I haven't written and told stories. When I'm not writing, I'm dreaming about writing, doing something wild and adventurous, or trying to make the world a better and more open-minded place to live in. I adore beautiful men, and I know I'm not alone in this! Eroticism between consenting adults, in all its many forms, is the icing on the cake of life!

www.ingramcontent.com/pod-product-compliance
Lightning Source LLC
Chambersburg PA
CBHW060821120626
46557CB00001B/308